COVENANT WITH EARTH

A Selection from the Poetry of

LEW SARETT

LEW SARETT

COVENANT WITH EARTH

A Selection from the Poetry of
LEW SARETT

INCLUDING SIX POEMS
NOT PREVIOUSLY PUBLISHED

SELECTED AND ARRANGED
BY
ALMA JOHNSON SARETT

WITH A FOREWORD BY
CARL SANDBURG

GAINESVILLE
UNIVERSITY OF FLORIDA PRESS
1956

MANY, MANY MOONS

COPYRIGHT, 1920, BY HENRY HOLT AND COMPANY
COPYRIGHT, 1948, BY LEW SARETT

THE BOX OF GOD

COPYRIGHT, 1922, BY HENRY HOLT AND COMPANY
COPYRIGHT, 1950, BY LEW SARETT

SLOW SMOKE

COPYRIGHT, 1925, BY HENRY HOLT AND COMPANY
COPYRIGHT, 1953, BY LEW SARETT

WINGS AGAINST THE MOON

COPYRIGHT, 1931, BY HENRY HOLT AND COMPANY
COPYRIGHT TRANSFERRED TO ALMA JOHNSON SARETT, 1955

COLLECTED POEMS

COPYRIGHT, 1941, BY HENRY HOLT AND COMPANY
COPYRIGHT TRANSFERRED TO ALMA JOHNSON SARETT, 1955

COVENANT WITH EARTH

COPYRIGHT, 1956, BY ALMA JOHNSON SARETT

First Printing

*Library of Congress Catalogue
Card No. 56-12859*

UNIVERSITY OF FLORIDA PRESS

PRINTED BY THE RECORD PRESS, INC.
ST. AUGUSTINE, FLORIDA

FOR

LLOYD

NICOLE

MARY

and WENDY

WITH THANKS—

Although I assume full responsibility for the selection and arrangement of the poems in this book, I acknowledge with gratitude the generous help of Carl Sandburg, John T. Frederick, Cornelius Carman Cunningham, Don Geiger, Allen O. Skaggs, Jr., and Inez and Clark Weaver; and of my husband's children, Lewis Hastings Sarett and Helen Sarett Stockdale.

To Carl Sandburg I am also indebted for permission to use the slightly modified version of the Foreword he wrote for the *Collected Poems of Lew Sarett*.

ALMA JOHNSON SARETT

October, 1956
Gainesville, Florida

CONTENTS

I

FLIGHT OVER DECOYS

    * *Previously unpublished.*

II

BENEATH A BENDING FIR

III

THUNDERDRUMS AND CEDAR FLUTE

A. *The Box of God*

* *Previously unpublished.*

FOREWORD

Books say Yes to life. Or they say No. *Covenant with Earth*, a selection from the poems of Lew Sarett, says Yes.

Picking classics in contemporary books is like picking winners in baseball or durable forms of government among nations. One man's guess is as good as another's.

We might say, "Herewith is entered Lew Sarett and his poetry as a runner for a place among the classics." And it would be only a guess.

However, there is nothing in the stipulations of the Espionage Act nor in the Code of Chesterfield nor in the Marquis of Queensberry rules, that stops us from asking:

"Why not the loam and the lingo, the sand and the syllables of North America in the books of North America?"

And so Sarett . . . with tall timbers, fresh waters, blue ducks, and a loon in him. The loon, a poet's bird for sure, is here. Unless there is a loon cry in a book the poetry is gone out of it. We have too many orderly, respectable, synthesized poets in the United States and England. In their orientation with the library canary fed from delicatessen tins, they are strangers to the loon that calls off its long night cry in tall timber up among the beginnings of the Mississippi.

Lew Sarett had equipment. Years a forest ranger and a woodsman, other years a wilderness guide, companion of red and white men as an outrider of civilization, university professor, headline performer on the American platform, he brought wisdom of things silent and things garrulous to his books. Old men with strong heads and shrewd slow tongues, young men with tough feet, the wishing song of mate for mate—they are here. The loam and the lingo, the sand and the syllables of North America are here. The poetry of Lew Sarett says Yes.

CARL SANDBURG

INTRODUCTION

The roots of America strike deep into a rich earth, into the soil of a vast and varied wilderness. It was once, and in many respects is still, a dramatic expanse of brooding mountains and forests, of fertile Southern river-bottoms and stony New England hills, of plains and seas whose horizons challenge the imagination.

Men are shaped much by the soil on which they live, by the latitude, the formation, and the fertility of the region that sustains them. Their lives are affected profoundly by their environment of rivers and forests, by prevailing floods and drouths, by wind and weather—by nature. The character of the American draws its color and strength largely from the wild earth of America. It is no accident that the dominant traits of the American are his independence, his individualism, his forthrightness, his rebellion against restraints, and his passion for freedom. These are in part the effects of definite causes that lie in the character of our land.

Inevitably, therefore, the story of our country is largely an heroic tale of the soil and of the folk who derive their vitality from the earth. It is a thrilling record of the ventures of fur-traders and voyageurs, of cowpunchers and prospectors, of farmers and railway builders and loggers, who hurled themselves at the gigantic barriers of mountains and deserts and forests; of pioneers who fought toe to toe with every form of adversity which nature can devise; who finally subdued a stubborn land and established an amazing nation.

Many of us in this nation are moved deeply by that drama of the frontiers, by the past and present glory of rural America. We are interested in the brute and human creatures who have played—and are playing—roles in that epical conquest, in the buffalo, the bear, and the coyote, in the cowhand, the ranger, and the farmer, in the lumberjack, the French-Canadian coureur de bois, and the Indian.

No doubt some Americans, urban and sophisticated, regard these rural regions and folk as remote in time and in geography—and of no great consequence. How amusing an attitude like this, when one considers that the United States is overwhelmingly agrarian in its expanse and in the source of its strength. Others of us, however, feel that these regions and their earthy folk are of great moment: they represent a precious inheritance; the remnants of them are a vital part of the life of our country today; they give America much of her peculiar identity, color, and power; and they are in the blood of America. Indeed, some of us think that these are all that matter much—the wild earth, nature: the enduring mountains that look down imperturbably on the human race, on its troubles, its momentary triumphs, its passing vanities; the permanent, fecund earth which yields up its fruit century on century and sustains the brute and human life of the world. We love the solid companionship of the simple folk of the soil, who, unlike their clever, urban brothers, are candid, predictable, and robust of spirit; who are sturdy and wear well; who are producers and not parasites in our economic life; who are energizers and not devitalizers in the blood-stream of America. And a few of us are convinced that nature holds most of the answers to the big basic questions of life, that nature holds much of whatever in life is touched with joy, meaning, and beauty.

Feeling thus deeply, we devote our lives to these matters. Some of us dedicate ourselves in our vocations and our recreations to forest life or to the sea, to gardening or to farm life, to exploring woods and waters, or to discovering the rich resources of the wilderness. Others of us commit ourselves to scientific research into the ways of nature in order to unravel her mysteries and to tap the unplumbed reservoirs of power within her. And a few of us set out to devote our lives to re-creating for others the beauty of wild America; to writing much and to speaking much of American backwoods and frontiers, of wolves and deer and bear, of loggers and voyageurs and Indians.

Hence this collection of poems. It is the outgrowth of many years of life on the vanishing frontiers of the Rocky Mountains and of the forests of the Lake Superior region. It is an expression—however inadequate—of the feeling that much of whatever is joyous and significant in life, timeless, true, and peculiarly American, tends to be rooted in the wild earth of America.

Moving in and out of the old and new frontiers is one bronze figure not clearly understood by many of us—the American Indian. In certain groups of poems in this collection I have tried to capture the essence of this primitive American, especially the poetry implicit in his character, his life, and his modes of expression, in his songs, his dances, and his ceremonies, in his council-oratory, his legends, and his religion. In many other groups I have sought to capture the poetry in some of the white characters of our remote borderlands, in mountaineers, plainsmen, and woodsmen, and in the wild creatures of our wilderness. These latter borderland folk are somewhat familiar types to most readers. One may write of white frontiersmen and wild animals with the confidence that the reader will bring to one's writings a more or less adequate background of information concerning their places in the American scene and their ways of life. Therefore, the groups of poems which deal with the mountains of the West and the forests of the North, with the white backwoods folk and wild creatures who move through them, make no uncommon demands on the reader; they require no special pleading. One does not need to supplement them with an Appendix or an Introduction. The fact that I shall not discuss in these supplementary sections the many poems on white pioneers, on wild animals, and on nature does not imply a lack of concern with them. On the contrary, backwoods folk, wild creatures, and nature concern me profoundly. They explain in part the Indian who walks through many of the pages of this book: they are an integral part of his life; they are his antagonists and his protagonists; they shape his character. More than this, these white characters and wild creatures are important in their own right: they are bound up with the spectacular past of our nation and to a large extent with its virile present; they lie at the core of our history; they are intensely American characters in an intensely American scene. But they are closer to the currents of our lives than is the Indian. The poems of the frontier and nature, therefore, demand no out of the ordinary background; they may stand on their own legs. But a few of the Indian pieces—not all, by any means—require supplementary information. Hence this explanatory Introduction and the subsequent Appendix. I offer them with the thought that these—with the poems on which they bear—may enable the reader to grasp more readily the nature of the red man and of his life as they are treated in this book.

It is impossible, of course, to tell the whole story of the Original American in a collection of poems, an Introduction and a brief Appendix. It is possible, however, in this limited space to provide technical information on Indian practices and beliefs which may throw light on some of the poems and may help to build a somewhat better understanding of the Indian, and especially of the poetry in him—my chief concern in the Indian studies.

In many respects the red man is a personality and symbol peculiarly American. He plays a role in nearly every tale of American frontiers. He is bound up with our traditions. He warrants attention for what he is even today: for the complex social and economic problem created by the three hundred sixty thousand Indians in the United States; and for the real contribution the Indian is making to our arts. Assuredly, we should strive to understand this Original American and to preserve in our traditions the aboriginal color, character, and culture which are rapidly vanishing under the pressure of white civilization. Indeed, we must understand him if we are to understand our own origin as a nation.

Yet the average American gives little thought to the Indian of the past fifty years. He regards him as a remote creature, monosyllabic, sullen, unfathomable. He may picture him romantically: the circus type of Indian dressed in buckskin and eagle plumes, dangling at his waist bloody scalps, with upraised battle-ax stalking his white enemies in the forest—a picture that might have been true of an occasional Indian of a century ago. Or, somewhat familiar with the modern red man, he may imagine him with stark realism as struggling desperately for survival on his reservations, the dupe of cunning white men, ravaged by tuberculosis and trachoma, tattered, famished, frustrated, eking out a gaunt living by scratching the earth for a few potatoes or a handful of corn. Obviously, both pictures are extreme. The Indian is neither of these types—and he is both. He is at once crass and beautiful, mercenary and idealistic, amusing and tragic. But at all times he is full of the stuff of poetry.

Although the life of the North American Indian shines with the gold of poetry, he has no definite form of expression called "poetry." His poetry is implicit in his songs, in his dances, in his religion, and in his mode of expressing himself in council-talks, invocations, and ceremonies. The specific words which he utters in a song may be few. A literal interpretation of the words of a song or ritual, therefore, will rarely reveal the freight of ideas and beauty in the song or ceremony. For example, the only words expressed in a meaningful Chippewa war-dance may be the following:

> I am dancing in the sky,
> I am dancing in the sky
> With the scalp of a Cut-throat.

But the few words may imply much. In his songs and dances the Indian habitually suggests his ideas rather than states them explicitly. The few words uttered usually represent the peak of an emotional or an imaginative flight. If these words are supplemented by an understanding of the accompanying ritual, symbols, dance steps, and pantomime, and by knowledge of Indian legends, superstitions, and reli-

xviii

gion, the fragmentary phrases of the song may suggest a wealth of ideas and beauty.

The Indian themes in Part III, Flying Moccasins, Many Moons, and Red Gods, are therefore in no sense literal interpretations of aboriginal songs, dances, and rituals. They are not even approximate interpretations. They are original poems. They are based on typical, fragmentary Indian utterances in Indian ceremonies, which I strive to interpret and amplify in the light of aboriginal beliefs and practices. They are efforts to dramatize more explicitly in the English language ideas and feelings merely suggested by Indian originals.

In this council-oratory, however, the Indian is more prodigal of language, more explicit, and more didactic. Consequently, the council-talk poems in Part III, Council-Fires, though still not translations, are closer to definite originals. Most of them are based on council-talks I have heard among the Chippewas. In these pieces I have tried faithfully to reproduce genuine Indian speech-situations and common Indian problems and issues; I have tried to capture faithfully Indian habits of thought and feeling and to translate them into genuine Indian idiom.

The Indian narratives and character studies in Part III, The Box of God and Tamarack Blue, are obviously in no respect translations or even interpretations. They are more or less objective studies of typical red men and women and of poignant situations in their primitive life.

In all the Indian poems in this book, however, I have tried to be faithful to the fundamental nature of the aboriginal American, and to preserve as accurately as possible his leg-

xix

ends and traditions, his outlook on life and on the universe, and his peculiar ways of expressing himself.

I have sought, moreover, to maintain consistently the point of view of the Indian of the past fifty years and of today, and not that of the romanticized red man of a century ago. I am concerned chiefly with the modern reservation Indian, in his transition from primitive wild life to the white man's civilization. I have tried to reveal the innumerable paradoxes of his life in the past few decades, with its strange marriage of the old and the new, of the bizarre and the beautiful, of paganism and Christianity, of the banal and the sublime.

The red man in his picturesque setting of teepees and travois, of thundering buffalos and ambushed prairie-schooners heaped with scalped dead, has gone the way of the flintlock. With this colorful savage has vanished much of the romance of our wild yesterdays. Yet in the life of the Indian of the past half century there is a beauty that is often more moving, and certainly more kaleidoscopic, than that of the old days of the war-dance. In this transitional type of Indian living on the modern reservation there is a rugged, earthy quality that is distinctive of the New World. About this bronze figure, the symbol of our vanishing West, hovers an atmosphere as American as the fragrance of burning pine.

Beneath the often drab surface of the modern red man, there is an abundance of the crude ore of poetry. The ingredients of poetry are in his characteristic imagery, in his idiom, and in the mysticism that marks his religion. Power lies in the aboriginal rhythms that move him to pound his feet on the ground and to shout heavenward in the war-songs, ceremonies, and medicine-dances which he still preserves. Wistful beauty marks the minor melodies of the love songs which he plays on his cedar flute. His council-oratory is more than interesting in its mingling of banality and grandeur, of simplicity of utterance and sonorous rhetoric, of the mundane and the idealistic. His life is full of the rough elements of drama, of comedy, and of tragedy. Consider his desperate struggle of the past century to stem the tide of a bewildering, inexorable civilization whose inconsistencies he could not always grasp; to withstand the ravages of the white man's diseases to which he has not yet built up an immunity; to beat off the astute white swindlers who were ever ready to pounce upon him as wolves upon a wounded deer. In the drama enacted in our American wilderness he has played every role: hero and villain, hunter and hunted, victor and vanquished. Yesterday, defiant, imperious in his manner, gallantly he fought for his life with naked hands against storm and snow, against flood and fury, against man and beast and pestilence; heroically he fastened his fingers on the throat of a hostile world and forced it to yield up a living for himself, for his family, and for his tribe. Today, poverty-stricken, more or less broken, stripped of much of his former high color and grandeur, he is making his exit in the West and the North, fading in the dusk and darkness of oblivion.

And oblivion it is, in the opinion of many of us, notwithstanding the apparent increase in the Indian population of the United States in the past fifty years. Some of us feel that the numerical increase is misleading, for it represents additional mixed-bloods—the result of the infusion of white blood. The number of full-blooded pagan Indians, of Indians of pure racial type, in many tribes—not all—is steadily decreasing.

In all this time and trouble, when the red man was driven

from pillar to post, he had but one powerful friend, except for the occasional white missionary: the United States Bureau of Indian Affairs in the Department of the Interior. And even this agency for good often gave a sorry account of its guardianship. It is only in recent years that the Office of Indian Affairs has attacked the Indian problem consistently with intelligence, sympathy, and vision.

Again, consider the dramatic religious struggle which still goes on in the hearts of many of the older Indians today as they strive naively to reconcile in their lives two irreconcilable religions, Christianity and paganism; to follow concurrently monotheism and animism. My mind goes back to Alex Down-wind, who rang the church bell zealously on Sunday morning and worshiped God devoutly in the little Christian mission on the pine-clad bluffs overlooking Lake Superior, but who on Sunday night retired furtively to the dark woods two miles from the Indian village to his medicine-lodge to conjure the evil spirits to his side. I can still see him in the firelight, chanting, beating his drum, invoking the evil spirits to help him make potent medicine for the assembled Indians—for a consideration: medicine to paralyze the limbs of an enemy; medicine to enable a young man to seduce a loved one; medicine to enable a woman to commune with the spirit of her dead husband. Can these religions be reconciled? An old Indian can reconcile them—somehow.

The musical expression of the aboriginal American, however cacophonous to white ears, contains poetry. The starkly elemental, and sometimes profoundly stylized, dances, in which the pagan elder folk—and many of the young—for a moment dance their way out of their rags and realism back to the splendor of another day, or into the lofty realm of the spirit which many Indians attain even today—these hold moments of power and beauty.

Dignity, economy of word, vivid imagery, and irony distinguish his council-speaking. His deliberative speeches sometimes rise to great heights.

Imagination and fervor color his rituals and his religion. His animistic interpretations of the phenomena of nature are complex and complete in their personification of earth and sky and water, of beast and bird and reptile, of the flash of lightning, the rumble of thunder, and the roar of big winds. Indian metaphysics may strike the white man as preposterous; nevertheless, the red man's interpretation of the universe and of man's place in it is on the whole big, sweeping, and bold in its scope and contours, and certainly to the minds of the older Indians it is more real, immediate, and compelling than the white man's explanation of life. Mysticism and a dreadful reality and imminence mark the supernatural world in which the so-called pagan Indian lives. He walks through life every day, every hour, communing with the spirits that reside in pine and eagle and star, ever invoking the ghosts of the evil and the ghosts of the good who crowd the dark universe. We smile patronizingly at some of his elemental notions, but the Indian possessed a religion that was terribly real to him; and he really worked at his religion—seven days of the week.

The life of the aboriginal American is not wholly somber; it has its high lights of humor and comedy. Grotesquery crops up in some of his attempts to adapt himself to the white man's mode of living with its baffling machines and its incomprehensible customs. Incongruity often marks his culture—even the furnishings of his wigwam or cabin, with its agglomeration of beaded buckskin medicine-bags and alarm clocks, of papoose cradle-boards and cosmetic jars, of stone pestles and mortars and battered phonographs. I am reminded of the old Chippewa buck who was given by the government title in fee simple to a tract of one hundred sixty acres of choice Minnesota pine, which was to be his home thereafter. He traded his valuable homestead—all that he possessed in the world—to a conscienceless white man for a team of black horses with glittering silver harness and a shining black hearse with plate glass windows and blowing black plumes. Proudly he drove the horses hitched to the hearse back to the Chippewa village in order to impress his neighbors. And within the hearse, behind the glass windows, in place of a coffin, squatted his ample squaw beaming and bowing right and left. The incident was amusing? Yes—and tragic. It illustrates a trait too common in Indians once upon a time. But there are few Indians as gullible and childlike as these Indians nowadays. The red man has learned his lessons in the school of bitter experience.

One finds much of interest in the dialectic novelty of his speech. The pidgin-English of the woods Indians on the Canadian border is an odd hybrid language in which the simple beauty of original Indian idiom is now shot through with twisted frontier slang and French-Canadian patois.

The drollness and comedy of the Indian of the past half century—rooted largely in anachronism and paradox—is epitomized perhaps by the incongruous costume he sometimes wears in impressive ceremonial dances: a nondescript outfit of beaded buckskin moccasins and the woolen underdrawers of the white man, a gaudy satin shirt and eagle plumes, sleigh-bells at his ankles or knees and a beaded medicine-bag in his hands.

Indeed, most of what is amusing, poignant, and tragic in the red man of the past few decades grows out of the unresolved clash of two civilizations in him, of two opposed cultures. In a few more years the conflict will be resolved. One civilization, one culture, will dominate the red man. It will be the white man's. The Indian, as a pure racial type and as a spectacular aboriginal figure, will be merged with the white American in mind and heart, in ritual and daily routine. He will exist only in the traditions of America as a dramatic personality, as an arresting American character of our heroic past.

It is the poetry of this relatively modern but vanishing type of reservation Indian which I wish to preserve in the Indian themes in Part III, sections A, B, C, D, and E, of this book. In the remaining groups I have tried to capture the spirit of the Indian's—and white man's—background of wild nature and of the creatures, four-footed and two-footed, who dwell in the backwoods and borderlands of our country.

Despite a persistent effort to record these matters objectively, it may be that one's report is colored by one's feelings and by what one is as a human being. In narrating facts it is difficult to avoid betraying one's human reactions to the facts —even if it were desirable. What a man is necessarily colors every line of what he writes. Therefore, in a book of this character one inevitably writes oneself down collaterally as a human being, for good or for ill.

In any event, I have written this collection of poems on the mountains, the deserts, and the forests of America, and on the brute and human folk who range its wilderness, because I feel that these aspects of American life should contain for Americans some degree of meaning. I have written about these simple folk of the earth, moreover, because I have lived with them, I know them, I find pleasure in their companionship, and my spirit belongs to them. Lastly, I have written about them because it gives me joy to write about them.

If this collection of poems, therefore, conveys to others a slight measure of the wild beauty of America, of her mountain ways and forest life, and if in some degree it gives others pleasure, I shall be glad. If it does not thus succeed—it was Walter Savage Landor who said, "There is delight in singing, though none hear beside the singer."

LEW SARETT.

PART I

FLIGHT OVER DECOYS

TO A WILD GOOSE OVER DECOYS

O lonely trumpeter, coasting down the sky,
Like a winter leaf blown from the bur-oak tree
By whipping winds, and flapping silverly
Against the sun—I know your lonely cry.

I know the worn wild heart that bends your flight
And circles you above this beckoning lake,
Eager of neck, to find the honking drake
Who speaks of reedy refuge for the night.

I know the sudden rapture that you fling
In answer to our friendly gander's call—
Halloo! Beware decoys!—or you will fall
With a silver bullet whistling in your wing!

Beat on your weary flight across the blue!
Beware, O traveller, of our gabbling geese!
Beware this weedy counterfeit of peace! . . .
Oh, I was once a passing bird like you.

GRANITE

O stolid granite hills, that tower serene
Above the world, its high concerns and mean,
Stoic before the wincing eyes, the rain
Of futile tears from multitudes in pain—
Knowing that this day's troubled flesh will pass
To spent dust under the impersonal grass—
Build in me, hills, the granite of your heart
That I may bear what rives my flesh apart;
Breed me as imperturbable and mute
To wretchedness as any stony butte;
Let fall your cowl of calm blue dusk on me,
The mantle of your cool tranquillity.

FOUR LITTLE FOXES

Speak gently, Spring, and make no sudden sound;
For in my windy valley, yesterday I found
New-born foxes squirming on the ground—
        Speak gently.

Walk softly, March, forbear the bitter blow;
Her feet within a trap, her blood upon the snow,
The four little foxes saw their mother go—
        Walk softly.

Go lightly, Spring, oh, give them no alarm;
When I covered them with boughs to shelter them from
    harm,
The thin blue foxes suckled at my arm—
        Go lightly.

Step softly, March, with your rampant hurricane;
Nuzzling one another, and whimpering with pain,
The new little foxes are shivering in the rain—
        Step softly.

HANG ME AMONG YOUR WINDS

Hang me among your winds, O God,
Above the tremulous stars,
Like a harp of quivering silver strings,
Showering, as it swings,
Its tuneful bars
Of eerie music on the earth.

Play over me, God,
Your cosmic melodies:
The gusty overture for Spring's
Caprice and wayward April's mirth;
The sensuous serenade
Of summer, languid in the alder glade;
The wistful symphonies
Of Autumn; and Winter's rhapsodies
Among the drifted dunes—
Her lullabies and her torrential tunes
Moody with wild cadenzas, with fitful stress
And poignant soundlessness.

Touch me, O God, with but a gesture—
And let each finger sweep
Over my strings until they leap
With life, and rain
Their silver chimes upon the plain,
In harmonies of far celestial spaces,
Of high and holy places.

FEUD

Poor wayworn creature! O sorely harried deer,
What drove you, quivering like a poplar-blade,
To refuge with my herd? What holds you here
Within my meadow, broken and afraid?

Tilting your nose to tainted air, you thrill
And freeze to wailing wolves! Fear you the sound
Of the coyotes eager for a tender kill?
Or yet the baying of the hunter's hound?

Let fall your anguish, harried one, and rest;
Bed yourself down among your kin, my cattle;
Sleep unperturbed, no spoiler shall molest
You here this night, for I shall wage your battle.

There was a day when coyotes in a pack,
Wolves of another hue, another breed,
With Christ upon their lips, set out to track
Me down and drop me, for my blood, my creed.

O hunted creature, once I knew the thud
Of padded feet that put you into flight,
The bugle-cry, suffused with lust for blood,
That trembled in the brazen bell of night.

I knew your frenzied rocky run, the burst
Of lungs, the rivers of fire in every vein;
I knew your foaming lip, your boundless thirst,
The rain of molten-hammering in your brain.

Bide with me then, against the wolves' return,
For I shall carry on the feud for you;
And it shall be, to me, of small concern
If the wolf-hearts walk on four soft feet or two.

Oh, let them come! And I shall burn their flanks
With a blast of hell to end their revelry,
And whistle molten silver through their ranks,
Laughing—one round for you and one for me.

BIRD'S-EYE

The valley spread below Bald Eagle Pass
A miniature world, a sweep of mountain-view;
The firs as thick and soft as blades of grass
And lakes of luminous blue.

Fragments the waters seemed—as if the bowl
Of sky had fallen from the hands of God,
And shattering itself upon a knoll,
Lay littered on the sod.

ANGUS McGREGOR

Angus McGregor lies brittle as ice,
　　With snow tucked up to his jaws,
Somewhere tonight where the hemlocks moan
　　And crack in the wind like straws.

Angus went cruising the woods last month,
　　With a blanket-roll on his back,
With never an ax, a dirk, a gun,
　　Or a compass in his pack.

"The hills at thirty below have teeth;
　　McGregor," I said, "you're daft
To tackle the woods like a simple child."
　　But he looked at me and laughed.

He flashed his teeth in a grin and said:
　　"The earth is an open book;
I've followed the woods for forty years,
　　I know each cranny and crook.

"I've battled her weather, her winds, her brutes,
　　I've stood with them toe to toe;
I can beat them back with my naked fist
　　And answer them blow for blow."

Angus McGregor sleeps under the stars,
　　With an icicle gripped in his hand,
Somewhere tonight where the grim-lipped peaks
　　Brood on a haggard land.

Oh, the face of the moon is dark tonight,
  And dark the gaunt wind's sigh;
And the hollow laughter troubles me
  In the wild wolves' cry.

LET ME GO DOWN TO DUST

Let me go down to dust and dreams
Gently, O Lord, with never a fear
Of death beyond the day that is done;
In such a manner as beseems
A kinsman of the wild, a son
Of stoic earth whose race is run.
Let me go down as any deer,
Who, broken by a desperate flight,
Sinks down to slumber for the night—
Dumbly serene in certitude
That it will rise again at dawn,
Buoyant, refreshed of limb, renewed,
And confident that it will thrill
Tomorrow to its nuzzling fawn,
To the bugle-notes of elk upon the hill.

Let me go down to dreams and dust
Gently, O Lord, with quiet trust
And the fortitude that marks a child
Of earth, a kinsman of the wild.
Let me go down as any doe
That nods upon its ferny bed,
And, lulled to slumber by the flow
Of talking water, the muffled brawl
Of far cascading waterfall,
At last lets down its weary head
Deep in the brookmints in the glen;
And under the starry-candled sky,
With never the shadow of a sigh,
Gives its worn body back to earth again.

FRAIL BEAUTY

O molten dewdrop, trembling in the light
  Of dawn, and clinging to the brookmint-blade—
  A pendent opal on a breast of jade—
How came your splendor, so limpid and so bright?
How your clear symmetry? And what weird sleight
  Of art suffused you with each rainbow-shade,
  Captured your evanescent hour, and made
A quivering soul from fire and mist and night?

Fleeting your span! Yet I shall be content
  To let the Cosmic Power that built in you
Such frail wet beauty, such luster opulent,
  And such immortal life as lies in dew,
Fashion the fragile moment of my soul
In what frail shape It deems a perfect whole.

THE WORLD HAS A WAY WITH EYES

To Helen S.

Untroubled your eyes, O child, as ingenuous
And virginal as dew, as clear and clean,
Tranquil as mountain pools that hold the blue
    Of sky with never a blur between.

But there may come a day when ominous clouds
Will sully them; when the world's craft will touch
Their deeps and put in them the glint that lurks
    In the eyes of those who know too much.

The world has a way with eyes. Oh, eyes there are:
Eyes that forlornly fawn like mongrel dogs;
Or move as suavely as silt in a beaver-dam
    Flows over treacherous sunken logs;

Eyes that are cobwebbed windows in a house,
Deserted, bleak, where a soul once lived, and fled,
Behind whose drawn green shutters slippered ghosts
    Conjure among the diffident dead;

Men's eyes more cold than the stones in Pilate's skull;
Or as wistfully patient as the Crucified;
Eyes that are sullen ponds in whose dark depth
    Sinister green-lipped fishes glide.

Oh, the world has a way with eyes. Cling to me, child,
Here where the mountains surge to immaculate blue,

Where the winds blow pure and cool and the eagle soars;
Let the wild sweet earth have its way with you.

Keep a long, long look on pine and peak that rise
Serene today, tomorrow—when the world's eyes go
To socketed dust; keep a long look on the hills.
They know something, child, they know.

THE LOON

A lonely lake, a lonely shore,
A lone pine leaning on the moon;
All night the water-beating wings
Of a solitary loon.

With mournful wail from dusk to dawn
He gibbered at the taunting stars—
A hermit-soul gone raving mad,
And beating at his bars.

LET ME FLOWER AS I WILL

God, let me flower as I will!
For I am weary of the chill
Companionship of cloistered vines
And hothouse-nurtured columbines;
Oh, weary of the pruning-knife
That shapes my prim decorous life—
Of clambering trellises that hold me,
Of flawless patterned forms that mold me.

God, let me flower as I will!
A shaggy rambler on the hill—
Familiar with April's growing pain
Of green buds bursting after rain.
Oh, let me hear among the sheaves
Of autumn, the song of wistful leaves,
The lullaby of the brook that dallies
Among the high blue mountain valleys.
And may my comrades be but these:
Birds on the bough, and guzzling bees
Among my blossoms, as they sup
On the dew in my silver-petaled cup.

God, let my parching roots go deep
Among the cold green springs, and keep
Firm grip upon the mossy edges
Of imperishable granite ledges,
That thus my body may withstand
The avalanche of snow and sand,
The trample of the years, the flail
Of whipping wind and bouncing hail.

And when December with its shroud
Of fallen snow and leaden cloud,
Shall find me in the holiday
Of slumber, shivering and gray
Against the sky—and in the end,
My somber days shall hold no friend
But a whimpering wolf, and on the tree
A frozen bird—so may it be.
For in that day I shall have won
The glory of the summer sun;
My leaves, by windy fingers played,
An eerie music shall have made;
I shall have known in some far land
The tender comfort of a Hand,
And the liquid beauty of a Tongue
That finds its syllables among
Wild wind and waterfall and rill—
God, let me flower as I will!

THE GRANITE MOUNTAIN

To Carl Sandburg

I know a mountain, lone it lies
Under wide blue Arctic skies.

Gray against the crimson rags
Of sunset loom its granite crags.

Gray granite are the peaks that sunder
The clouds, and gray the shadows under.

Down the weathered gullies flow
Waters from its crannied snow:

Tumbling cataracts that roar
Cannonading down the shore;

And rivulets that hurry after
With a sound of silver laughter.

Up its ramparts winds a trail
To a clover-meadowed vale,

High among the hills and woods
Locked in lonely solitudes.

Only wild feet can essay
The perils of that cragged way.

And here beneath the rugged shoulders
Of the granite cliffs and boulders,

In the valley of the sky
Where tranquil twilight shadows lie,

Hunted creatures in their flight
Find a refuge for the night.

MESA-MIST

When the passion of the day is done,
And the weary sun,
Lingering above the calm plateau
And mesa-waters, stains
The cottonwoods and sleeping cranes
With afterglow,
Day keeps a fleeting tryst
With Night in the mesa-mist.
When her crimson arm embraces
The clouds and plains
No more, spent Day slips quietly to rest
On a ghostly breast—
And nothing remains,
Save in the twilit places,
The ghosts of rains
And columbines whose wistful faces
Droop where the purple-pollened fir
Tinctures the dusk with lavender.

REQUIEM FOR A MODERN CROESUS

To him the moon was a silver dollar, spun
Into the sky by some mysterious hand; the sun
Was a gleaming golden coin—
His to purloin;
The freshly minted stars were dimes of delight
Flung out upon the counter of the night.

In yonder room he lies,
With pennies on his eyes.

DUST

This much I know:
Under the bludgeonings of snow
And sleet and sharp adversity,
From high estate
The seemingly immortal tree
Shall soon or late
Go down to dust;
When a wild wet gust
Tumbles the gaunt debris
Down from the gashed plateau
And out upon the plain,
The dust shall go
Down with the rain;
Rivers are slow,
Rivers are fast,
But rivers and rains run down to the sea,
All rains go down to the sea at last.

Oh, shake the red bough,
And cover me now,
Cover me now with dreams,
With a blast
Of falling leaves, with the filtered gleams
Of the moon;
Shake the dead bough
And cover me now,
For soon
Rivers and rains shall go with me
Down to the vast infinity.

GOD IS AT THE ANVIL

God is at the anvil, beating out the sun;
    Where the molten metal spills,
    At His forge among the hills
He has hammered out the glory of a day that is done.

God is at the anvil, welding golden bars;
    In the scarlet-streaming flame
    He is fashioning a frame
For the shimmering silver beauty of the evening stars.

LOOK FOR ME

When the sinking sun
Goes down to the sea,
And the last day is done,
Oh, look for me
Beneath no shimmering monument,
Nor tablet eloquent
With a stiff decorous eulogy;
Nor yet in the gloom
Of a chipped and chiseled tomb.

But when the pregnant bud shall burst
With April's sun, and bloom
Upon the bough—
Look for me now,
In the sap of the first
Puccoon whose fragile root,
Bruised by the rain,
Has left a crimson stain
Upon the cedar-glade.

Oh, look for me then,
For I shall come again,
In the leopard-lily's shoot,
And in the green wet blade
Of the peppergrass.
When the warm winds pass
Over the waking rills,
And the wild arbutus spills
Its fragrance on the air—

Look for me then—
Asleep in a ferny glen
High in the hills,
Deep in the dew-drenched maiden-hair;
I shall be waiting, waiting there.

LITTLE ENOUGH THERE IS OF WORTH

Little enough there is of worth
On this green ball of earth:
Wind in a hemlock-tree, to shake
A cool wet music from the brake;
Flame in an earthen bowl
To warm a frozen soul
And cheer a heart grown chill
With solitude and ill;
And water in a rill,
Rimmed round with moss that drips
Upon the rock, until it fashions
A goblet for hot lips,
A cup for futile passions.

And when the high heart is broken,
The last word spoken,
And tears are many as the dew—
The fragmentary dreams
Of beauty that the world discloses
In every woodland, these are sweet,
My bread, my wine, my meat:
October smoke that hovers on the streams
And spirals up the blue;
Clambering mountain-roses,
By tender-fingered rain unfurled;
And honey-laden bees
That nuzzle the buds of shy anemones,
And dust a golden pollen on the world.

But rarer far than these—
Than any flower-cup or pool
From which to drink one's fill
Of loveliness, a potion beaded, cool,
To fortify the will—
I hold the sanguine hue
Of dawn, when courage springs anew
And the heart is high
As the banners of the day go up the sky;
The wine of the setting sun that holds
A promise of a glad tomorrow;
The pool of moonlight that enfolds
The sable hills and hollows—
As the quivering silver cry
Of a lost lone loon
Answers the drowsy swallow's,
And faintly the echoes die—
The pool of mountain moon
In which to fling oneself and make an
end of sorrow.

KINSMEN

A mountain pool is brother to the sky;
It mirrors every gray owl flapping by,
Holds on its silver all the traceries
Of clouds and overarching trees.

The wash of water and of wind is one;
And any lapsing pond gives back the sun,
Doubles the ragged scarlet in the west,
And holds the stars upon its breast.

Even as tranquil water in a hollow
Mirrors the fleeting shadow of a swallow,
Oh, even so am I content to be
Kinsman of sky and wind and sea.

MARCHING PINES

Up the drifted foothills,
　Like phantoms in a row,
The ragged lines of somber pines
　Filed across the snow.

Down the gloomy coulees
　The burdened troopers went,
Snowy packs upon their backs,
　Bowed of head and bent.

Up the cloudy mountains,
　A mournful singing band,
Marching aimless to some nameless,
　Undiscovered land.

COVENANT WITH EARTH

So! It is darkly written: I must go,
Go shadowed by sorrow as my father went,
Hurled in his highest moment earthward, spent,
Like a shattered falling arrow from a bow.

Oh, let it stand! No syllable of grief
Shall tremble on my lips, no teary brine
Dribble upon an open wound of mine.

Once having looked upon an autumn leaf,
Palsied and scourged, a soaring eagle slain,
And rose-leaves pelted down to dust by rain—
I came to understand the blind earth's way,
Her calm indifference to shattered clay,
Her will to tramp on flesh with the iron cleat
Of anguish, failure, bitterness, defeat.
As an intimate of earth I came to know
That this gaunt wretched moment long ago
Was written in my covenant with the soil;
That all who hold a lien on life contract
With the elemental earth to hold the pact
Subject to all its varied terms, its sweet,
Its bitter, its endless trouble and its toil.
Too well I came to know that a groan, a curse,
Shall never change the inexorable fact
That flesh must break, for better or for worse.

Hear me, O stern Inscrutable-One! Rough-hew
To a barbed and tortuous point whatever lance

Of pain you will, or of harrowing circumstance,
And plunge it through my ribs from out the blue.
The thrust shall find me dry-eyed, resolute,
Dropping no moan—whatever blood shall spill;
As imperturbable as any brute,
As taciturn as stone upon a hill.

PART II

BENEATH A BENDING FIR

DEEP WET MOSS

Deep wet moss and cool blue shadows
    Beneath a bending fir,
And the purple solitude of mountains,
    When only the dark owls stir—
Oh, there will come a day, a twilight,
    When I shall sink to rest
In deep wet moss and cool blue shadows
    Upon a mountain's breast,
And yield a body torn with passions,
    And bruised with earthly scars,
To the cool oblivion of evening,
    Of solitude and stars.

CATTLE BELLS

How clear tonight the far jang-jangling bells
Of Champlain's herd, the melody that wells
Tuneful as stony water, from the nook
   In the sweet-grass marsh of Alder Brook.

What patient strength of earth their tones disclose:
The peace of stars like quiet-falling snows,
Of forests slumbering, soundless, but for the fox
   Stepping among the clinking rocks.

What world unsullied, free of guile and snare,
What valley of contentment they declare:
A valley soothing as its bullfrog croak,
   Serene as the one slim drifting smoke;

A valley of waters that softly talk of dreams,
Of the slow sweet enterprises of little streams,
Of their solemn concern with every woodland thing
   Lingering to bathe a paw, a wing;

Of the veery, thick with sleep, who stretched his throat
And tossed in the brook a single pebbly note;
Of the frothing doe who buried her muzzle, drank,
   And dropped in the brookmints on the bank. . . .

I shall lie down and sleep . . . sleep now . . .
And yield to the cool bells this blazing brow—
Knowing grief will not stalk me, nor intrude
   Longer tonight upon my brood.

Now that the placid bells have given birth
To the gentle certainties of night and earth,
I shall lie down and sleep, sleep tranquilly;
   And trouble, trouble will fall from me.

IMPASSE

Six little sheep
Bleating in the sun,
Don't know which
Way they should run.

Fence to the left;
Fence to the right;
Before them a mouse
Stabs them with fright.

Nothing to do
But to wheel and go—
A little too much
For sheep to know.

THE LAMPS OF BRACKEN-TOWN

Beneath a canopy of ferns
The frosted berries hung;
Like lanterns on a slender arm,
Their blazing crimson swung—
Lanterns to rout the brooding dark,
To blaze the way of crickets
Adventuring down the gloomy streets
Beneath the bracken-thickets.

TO A GROVE OF SILVER BIRCHES

Good morning, lovely ladies! I've never seen
    You half so fair—I swear;
How beautiful your gowns of apple-green!
    And the ribbons in your hair!

What rapture do you await? What coming swain?
    Such rustling of petticoats!
Such wagging of heads and prinking in the rain!
    Such fluttering at your throats!

Dear winsome vestals, your flurry is no whim.
    I know your sly design;
And why the sap goes pulsing up each limb
    Sparkling as apple wine.

O ladies, trick you in your gala-best;
    For out of the ardent South,
Young April comes with a passion in his breast,
    And a kiss upon his mouth.

SO LIKE A QUIET RAIN

So like a rain she seems, a soothing rain
Tapping cool fingers on a window-pane,
And dropping syllables more slow and soft
Than the talk of sleepy pigeons in a loft.

FAMILIAR WINGS

Oh, I shall wait for you,
Among these tilting pines
That lock their marching lines
And lean their lances on the moon;
Wait for you here, like any loon
That mourns upon the white
Of moonlit water and shakes the night
With the trembling echoes of his sorrow;
Oh, I shall wait for you—
Tomorrow and tomorrow—
As any loon that rings
His anguish skyward tone by tone
May wait forlorn, alone,
For the coming music of sweet familiar wings.

CLOUDS AT TIMBERLINE

Blown by the gale, all day the low black clouds
    Rolled up the valley, billowy and immense,
And heaped themselves against the mountainside
    Like tumble-weeds upon a fence.

So high they piled, that soon they overflowed
    At Beartooth Pass, and rolled out on the plain
In a cloudy avalanche, like tumble-weeds
    Bouncing before a windy rain.

WHEN THE ROUND BUDS BRIM

When April showers stain
The hills with mellow rain,
The quaking aspen tree,
So delicate, so slim,
In glittering wet festoons,
Is a lovely thing to see—
When the round buds brim
And burst their fat cocoons,
Like caterpillars, clean,
And cool, and silver-green,
Uncurling on the limb.

And lovely when September,
With magic pigment dyes
The aspen stems with wings
Of flimsy butterflies—
When the frosted leaf swings
Its gold against the sun
And dances on the bough.

But when in bleak November
The latest web is spun,
And the gold has turned to dun—
When winds of winter call
And the bare tree answers
As the last leaves fall
Like crumpled moths—oh, now
How sad it is to look

Upon the leaves in the brook—
So many tattered hosts,
So many haggard ghosts,
So many broken dancers.

THE SHEEPHERDER

Loping along on the day's patrol,
I came on a herder in Madison's Hole;
Furtive of manner, blazing of eye,
He never looked up when I rode by;
But counting his fingers, fiercely intent,
Around and around his herd he went:

> *One sheep, two sheep, three sheep, four . . .*
> *Twenty and thirty . . . forty more;*
> *Strayed—nine ewes; killed—ten rams;*
> *Seven and seventy lost little lambs.*

He was the only soul I could see
On the lonely range for company—
Save a lean lone wolf and a prairie-dog,
And a myriad of ants at the foot of a log;
So I sat the herder down on a clod—
But his eyes went counting the ants in the sod:

> *One sheep, two sheep, three sheep, four . . .*
> *Fifty and sixty . . . seventy more;*
> *There's not in this flock a good bell-wether!*
> *Then how can a herder hold it together!*

Seeking to cheer him in his plight,
I flung my blankets down for the night;
But he wouldn't talk as we sat by the fire—
Corralling sheep was his sole desire;
With fingers that pointed near and far,
Mumbling, he herded star by star:

One sheep, two sheep, three—as before!
Eighty and ninety . . . a thousand more!
My lost little lambs—one thousand seven!—
Are wandering over the hills of Heaven.

ALMANACK

I

BLUE EARTH

Blue snow that mantles the dusky plain,
 Blue as a tempered blade;
Blue the air in the coulee-gloom,
 And blue the forest-shade.

Pallid the sun that wanly seeps
 Through a gash in the sodden cloud—
Tomorrow the firs will groan with snow
 And wear a winding-shroud.

II

HOLLOW NIGHT

Brittle the sky and hollow the earth,
 Hollow the frozen night,
Save for the boom of a brittle birch
 Crashing from its height.

And the tinkle of stars in the brittle sky
 Like clinking ice in a bowl—
Oh, coyote, sleep through another day
 Deep in your cragged hole.

III

DRY DAWN

A subtle flush on the morning's blue
A tinted delicate crimson hue,

As the blush on wild arbutus petals;
Haze on the marsh that swiftly settles;
Dewless the rushes, parched of root,
Falling to powder under foot
Like pasture puff-balls, scorched and dry
In the glittering noon of late July;
The rain-crow mourning under the leaf—
Soon he will know an end to his grief.

IV

STILL POOL

A still pool on a windless day
    That mirrors the falling leaf,
And mackerel clouds like wrinkled sand
    Riffling a silver reef;

A gust that shatters the glassy pond
    And drives it helter-skelter,
And shrieking gulls that ride the wind—
    Scurry now for shelter.

V

EARLY RAIN

Before gray daylight, ragged rain
Slanting down on the windowpane;
Out of the cloudburst, silver lances
Spearing the oak leaf while it dances—
The leaden sky will open soon,
The sun will show his face by noon.

THE GREAT DIVIDE

When I drift out on the Silver Sea,
O may it be
A blue night
With a white moon
And a sprinkling of stars in the cedar-tree;
And the silence of God,
And the low call
Of a lone bird. . . .

HOLLYHOCKS

I have a garden, but, oh, dear me!
What a ribald and hysterical company:
Incorrigible mustard, militant corn,
Frivolous lettuce, and celery forlorn;
Beets apoplectic and fatuous potatoes,
Voluptuous pumpkins and palpitant tomatoes;
Philandering pickles trysting at the gate,
Onions acrimonious, and peppers irate;
And a regiment of hollyhocks marching around them
To curb their mischief, to discipline and bound them.

Hollyhocks! Hollyhocks! What should I do
Without the morale of a troop like you!

Some lackadaisically yawn and nod;
Others, hypochondriac, droop on the sod:
Cabbage apathetic, parsnips sullen,
Peas downtrodden by the lancing mullein;
Boorish rutabagas, dill exotic,
The wan wax-bean, bilious and neurotic;
Dropsical melons, varicose chard,
And cauliflowers fainting all over the yard.
Thank heaven for the hollyhocks! Till day is done
They prod them to labor in the rain and the sun.

Hollyhocks! Hollyhocks! Stiff as starch!
Fix your bayonets! Forward! March!

FISHER OF STARS

My wild blood leaped as I watched the falling stars
    Flash through the night and gleam,
Like spawning trout that hurtle the riffled bars
    Of a dusky mountain stream.

Like quivering rainbow-trout that run in spring,
    Arching the water-slides—
Out of the limpid sky, in a wild wet fling,
    They shook their crimson sides.

My sportsman's heart flamed up, as the fishes dashed
    In school on shimmering school,
Through high cascades and waterfalls, and splashed
    In the deep of a cloudy pool.

I fished that pond; I chose my longest line,
    And cast with my supplest rod—
The one was a thing of dreams, oh, gossamer-fine;
    The other a gift from God.

I flicked the Milky Way from edge to edge
    With an iridescent fly;
I whipped the polar rapids, and every ledge
    And cut-bank in the sky.

To the Pleiades I cast with my willowy pole;
    And I let my line run out
To the farthest foamy cove and skyey hole—
    And I raised a dozen trout.

And every time one struck my slender hook,
    He shattered the trembling sea,
With a sweep of his shivering silver fin, and he shook
    A silver rain on me;

My line spun out, my fly-rod bent in twain,
    As over the sky he fought;
My fingers bled, my elbows throbbed with pain—
    But my fishing went for naught.

I landed never a one; my line and hackle
    Were none too subtle and fine;
For angling stars one wants more delicate tackle—
    A more cunning hand than mine.

BLACKTAIL DEER

The blacktail held his tawny marble pose,
With every supple muscle set to spring,
Nosing the tainted air—his slender limbs
And sinews like corded copper quivering.

Ponderous the minutes, while his smoldering eyes
Went burning over me, and searching mine;
His heart ticked off each moment as he stood
Waiting an ominous word, a sound, a sign.

I tossed a friendly gesture! The sinews snapped
And flung his bulk of rippled tawny stone
Over an alder, as when a bended pine,
Released from pressure, catapults a cone.

Bending an arch above the alder-crown,
In a stream of whistling wind the great buck went,
Flirting his tail in exclamation-marks
To punctuate his vast astonishment.

ARITHMETIC

To L. S. Jr.

Head bowed before the candle, and nose
   Plowing the stubborn soil
Of page on page of arithmetic
   He wriggles in his toil.

Tenaciously he strives to drag
   From its rocky tortuous nest
The elusive convolutioned length
   Of compound interest.

Grimly he grips an end of it,
   Like a robin, braced and firm,
Striving to tug from its lair in earth
   A slippery angle-worm.

TRAILING ARBUTUS

I found a wild arbutus in the dell,
The first-born blossom from the womb of spring;
The bud, unfurling, held me in a spell
With its hesitant awakening.

Fragrant its petals, pink and undefiled
As the palm of one new-born, or its finger-tips;
Delicate as the song of a little child,
And sweet as the breath between its lips.

Something in shy arbutus wet with dew
Lays hold of me, something I do not know—
Unless—among these blossoms once I knew
A little boy, oh, long ago.

WIND IN THE PINE

Oh, I can hear you, God, above the cry
Of the tossing trees—
Rolling your windy tides across the sky,
And splashing your silver seas
Over the pine,
To the water-line
Of the moon.
Oh, I can hear you, God,
Above the wail of the lonely loon—
When the pine-tops pitch and nod—
Chanting your melodies
Of ghostly waterfalls and avalanches,
Washing your wind among the branches
To make them pure and white.

Wash over me, God, with your piney breeze,
And your moon's wet-silver pool;
Wash over me, God, with your wind and night,
And leave me clean and cool.

A – THE BOX OF GOD *

I

BROKEN BIRD

O broken bird,
Whose whistling silver wings have known the lift
Of high mysterious hands, and the wild sweet music
Of big winds among the ultimate stars!—
The black-robed curés put your pagan Indian
Soul in their white man's House of God, to lay
Upon your pagan lips new songs, to swell
The chorus of amens and hallelujahs.
In simple faith and holy zeal, they flung
Aside the altar-tapestries, that you
Might know the splendor of God's handiwork,
The shining glory of His face. O eagle,
Crippled of pinion, clipped of soaring wing,
They brought you to a four-square box of God;
And they left you there to flutter against the bars
In futile flying, to beat against the gates,
To droop, to dream a little, and to die.

Ah, Joe Shing-ób—by the sagamores revered
As Spruce, the Conjurer, by the black-priests dubbed
The Pagan Joe—how clearly I recall
Your conversion in the Big-Knife's House of God,
Your wonder when you faced its golden glories.
Don't you remember?—when first you sledged from out

* For supplementary comments on this poem, and on other Indian themes, see *Appendix,* pages 145–167.

61

The frozen Valley of the Sleepy-eye,
And hammered on the gates of Fort Brazeau—
To sing farewell to Áh-nah-qúod, the Cloud,
Sleeping, banked high with flowers, clothed in the pomp
Of white man's borrowed garments, in the church?
Oh, how your heart, as a child's heart beating before
High wonder-workings, thrilled at the burial splendor!—
The coffin, shimmering-black as moonlit ice,
And gleaming in a ring of waxen tapers;
After the chant of death, the long black robes,
Blown by the wind and winding over the hills
With slow black songs to the marked-out-place-of-death;
The solemn feet that moved along the road
Behind the wagon-with-windows, the wagon-of-death,
With its jingling silver harness, its dancing plumes.
Oh, the shining splendor of that burial march,
The round-eyed wonder of the village throng!—
And oh, the fierce-hot hunger, the burning envy
That seared your soul when you beheld your friend
Achieve such high distinction from the black-robes!

And later, when the cavalcade of priests
Wound down from the fenced-in ground, like a slow black
    worm
Crawling upon the snow—don't you recall?—
The meeting in the mission?—that night, your first
In the white man's lodge of holy-medicine?
How clearly I can see your hesitant step
On the threshold of the church; within the door
Your gasp of quick surprise, your breathless mouth;
Your eyes round-white before the glimmering taper,

The golden-filigreed censer, the altar hung
With red rosettes and velvet soft as an otter's
Pelt in the frost of autumn, with tinsel sparkling
Like cold blue stars above the frozen snows.
Oh, the blinding beauty of that House of God!—
Even the glittering bar at Jock McKay's,
Tinkling with goblets of fiery devil's-spit,
With dazzling vials and many-looking mirrors,
Seemed lead against the silver of the mission.

I hear again the chanting holy-men,
The agents of the white man's Mighty Spirit,
Making their talks with strong, smooth-moving tongues:

"Hear! Hear ye, men of a pagan faith!
Forsake the idols of your heathen fathers,
The too-many ghosts that walk upon the earth;
For there lie pain and sorrow, yea, and death!

"Hear! Hear ye, men of a pagan faith!
And grasp the friendly hands we offer you
In kindly fellowship, warm hands and tender,
Yea, hands that ever give and never take.
Forswear the demon-charms of medicine-men;
Shatter the drums of conjuring Chée-sah-kée—
Yea, beyond these walls lie bitterness and death!

"Pagans!—ye men of a bastard birth!—bend;
Bow ye, proud heads, before this hallowed shrine!
Break!—break ye the knee beneath this roof,
For within this house lives God! Abide ye here.

Here shall your eyes behold His wizardry;
Here shall ye find an everlasting peace."

Ah, Joe the pagan, son of a bastard people,
Child of a race of vanquished, outlawed children,
Small wonder that you drooped your weary head,
Blinding your eyes to the suns of elder days;
For hungry bellies look for new fat gods,
And heavy heads seek newer, softer pillows.
With you again I hear the eerie chants
Floating from out the primal yesterdays—
The low sweet song of the doctor's flute, the slow
Resonant boom of the basswood water-drum,
The far voice of the fathers, calling, calling.
I see again the struggle in your eyes—
The hunted soul of a wild young grouse, afraid,
Trembling beneath maternal wings, yet lured
By the shrill whistle of the wheeling hawk.
I see your shuffling limbs, hesitant, faltering
Along the aisle—the drag of old bronzed hands
Upon your moccasined feet, the forward tug
Of others, soft and white, and very tender;
One forward step . . . another . . . a quick look back!—
Another step . . . another . . . and lo! the eyes
Flutter and droop before a flaming symbol,
The strong knees break before a blazoned altar
Glimmering its tapestries in the candle-light,
The high head beaten down and bending before
New wonder-working images of gold.

And thus the black-robes brought you into the house
Wherein they kept their God, a house of logs,

Square-hewn, and thirty feet by forty. They strove
To put before you food and purple trappings—
Oh, how they walked you up and down in the vestry
Proudly resplendent in your white man's raiment,
Glittering and gorgeous, the envy of your tribe:
Your stiff silk hat, your scarlet sash, your shoes
Shining and squeaking gloriously with newness!
Yet even unto the end—those blood-stained nights
Of the Sickness-on-the-lung; that bitter day
On the Barking-rock, when I packed you down from camp
At Split-hand Falls to the fort at Sleepy-eye;
While, drop by drop, your life went trickling out,
As sugar-sap that drips on the birch-bark bucket
And finally chills in the withered maple heart
At frozen dusk: even unto the end—
When the mission doctor, framed by guttering candles,
Hollowly tapped his hooked-horn finger here
And there upon your bony breast, like a wood-bird
Pecking and drumming on a rotten trunk—
Even unto this end I never knew
Which part of you was offering the holy prayers—
The chanting mouth, or the eyes that gazed beyond
The walls to a far land of windy valleys.
And sometimes, when your dry slow lips were moving
To perfumed psalms, I could almost, almost see
Your pagan soul aleap in the fire-light, naked,
Shuffling along to booming medicine-drums,
Shaking the flat black earth with moccasined feet,
Dancing again—back among the jangling
Bells and the stamping legs of gnarled old men—

Back to the fathers calling, calling across
Dead winds from the dim gray years.

O high-flying eagle,
Whose soul, wheeling among the sinuous winds,
Has known the molten glory of the sun,
The utter calm of dusk, and in the evening
The lullabies of moonlit mountain waters!—
The black-priests locked you in their House of God,
Behind great gates swung tight against the frightened
Quivering aspens, whispering perturbed in council,
And muttering as they tapped with timid fists
Upon the doors and strove to follow you
And hold you; tight against the uneasy winds
Wailing among the balsams, fumbling upon
The latch with fretful fingers; tight against
The crowding stars who pressed their troubled faces
Against the windows. In honest faith and zeal,
The black-robes put you in a box of God,
To swell the broken chorus of amens
And hallelujahs; to flutter against the door
Crippled of pinion, bruised of head; to beat
With futile flying against the gilded bars;
To droop, to dream a little, and to die.

II

WHISTLING WINGS

Shing-ób, companion of my old wild years
In the land of K'tchée-gah-mee, my good right arm
When we battled bloody-fisted in the storms

And snows with rotting scurvy, with hunger raw
And ravenous as the lusting tongues of wolves—
My Joe, no longer will the ghostly mountains
Echo your red-lunged laughters in the night;
The gone lone days when we communed with God
In the language of the waterfall and wind
Have vanished with your basswood water-drum.

Do you recall our cruise to Flute-reed Falls?
Our first together—oh, many moons ago—
Before the curés built the village mission?
How, banked against our camp-fire in the bush
Of sugar-maples, we smoked kín-nik-kin-ník,
And startled the somber buttes with round raw songs,
With wails that mocked the lynx who cried all night
As if her splitting limbs were torn with the pain
Of a terrible new litter? How we talked
Till dawn of the Indian's Kéetch-ie Má-ni-dó,
The Mighty Spirit, and of the white man's God?—
Don't you remember dusk at Cold-spring Hollow?—
The beaver-pond at our feet, its ebony pool
Wrinkled with silver, placid, calm as death,
Save for the fitful chug of the frog that flopped
His yellow jowls upon the lily-pad,
And the quick wet slap of the tails of beaver hurrying
Homeward across the furrowing waters, laden
With cuttings of tender poplar . . . down in the swale
The hermit-thrush who spilled his rivulet
Of golden tones into the purple seas
Of gloam among the swamps . . . and in the East,
Serene against the sky—do you remember?—

Slumbering Mont du Père, shouldering its crags
Through crumpled clouds, rose-flushed with afterglow . . .
And dew-lidded dusk that slipped among the valleys
Soft as a blue wolf walking in thick wet moss.
How we changed our ribald song for simple talk! . . .

"*My frien', Ah-déek, you ask-um plenty hard question:*
Ugh! w'ere Kéetch-ie Má-ni-dó he live?
W'ere all dose Eenzhun spirits walk and talk?
Me—I dunno! . . . Mebbe . . . mebbe over here,
In beaver-pond, in t'rush, in gromping bullfrog;
Mebbe over dere, he's sleeping in dose mountain. . . .

"*Sh-sh-sh! . . . Look!—over dere—look, my frien'!*
On Mont du Père—he's moving little! . . . ain't?
Under dose soft blue blanket she's falling down
On hill and valley! Somebody—somebody's dere!
In dose hill of Mont du Père, sleeping . . . sleeping . . ."

And when the fingers of the sun, lingering,
Slipped gently from the marble brow of the glacier
Pillowed among the clouds, blue-veined and cool,
How, one by one, like lamps that flicker up
In a snow-bound hamlet in the valley, the stars
Lighted their candles mirrored in the waters . . .
And floating from the hills of Sleepy-eye,
Soft as the wings of dusty-millers flying,
The fitful syllables of the Baptism River
Mumbling among its caverns hollowly,
Shouldering its emerald sweep through cragged cascades
In a flood of wafted foam, fragile, flimsy
As luna-moths fluttering on a pool . . .

"You hear dat, Caribou? . . . somebody's dere! . . .
Ain't?—in dose hills of Mont du Père—sleeping.
Sh-sh-sh! You hear dose far 'way Flute-reed Falls?
Somebody's dere in Mont du Père, sleeping . . .
Somebody he's in dere de whole night long . . .
And w'ile he's sleep, he's talking little . . . talking . . ."

Hush!—don't you hear K'tchée-gah-mee at midnight?—
That stretched far out from the banks of Otter-slide
To the dim wet rim of the world—South, East, West?—
The Big-water, calm, thick-flecked with the light of stars
As the wind-riffled fur of silver fox in winter . . .
The shuffle of the sands in the lapsing tide . . .
The slow soft wash of waters on the pebbles . . .

"Sh-sh-sh! . . . Look Ah-déek!—on K'tchée-gah-mee!
Somebody—somet'ing he's in dere . . . ain't? . . .
He's sleep w'ere black Big-water she's deep . . . Ho!
In morning he's jump up from hees bed and race
Wit' de wind; tonight he's sleeping . . . rolling little—
Dreaming about hees woman . . . rolling . . . sleeping . . ."

And later—you recall?—beyond the peaks
That tusked the sky like fangs of a coyote snarling,
The full-blown mellow moon that floated up
Like a liquid-silver bubble from the waters,
Serenely, till she pricked her delicate film
On the slender splinter of a cloud, melted,
And trickled from the silver-dripping edges.
Oh, the splendor of that night! . . . the Twin-fox stars
That loped across the pine-ridge . . . Red Ah-núng,

Blazing from out the cavern of the gloom
Like the smouldering coal in the eye of carcajou . . .
The star-dust in the valley of the sky,
Flittering like glow-worms in a reedy meadow! . . .

"Somebody's dere . . . He's walk-um in dose cloud . . .
You see-um? Look! He's mak'-um for bees woman
De w'ile she sleep, dose t'ing she want-um most—
Blue dress for dancing! You see, my frien'? . . . ain't?
He's t'rowing on de blanket of dose sky
Dose plenty-plenty handfuls of w'ite stars;
He's sewing on dose plenty teet' of elk,
Dose shiny looking-glass and plenty beads.
Somebody's dere . . . somet'ing he's in dere . . ."

Thus the green moons went—and many, many winters.
Yet we held together, Joe, until our day
Of falling leaves, like two split sticks of bur-oak
Lashed tight with buckskin buried in the bark.
Do you recollect our last long cruise together,
To Hollow-bear, on our line of beaver-traps?—
When cold Bee-bóan, the Winter-maker, hurdling
The rim-rock ridge, shook out his snowy hair
Before him on the wind and heaped up the hollows?—
Flanked by the drifts, our lean-to of toboggans,
Our bed of pungent balsam, soft as down
From the bosom of a wild gray goose in autumn . . .
Our steaming sledge-dogs buried in the snow-bank,
Nuzzling their snouts beneath their tented tails,
And dreaming of the paradise of dogs . . .
Our fire of pine-boughs licking up the snow,

And tilting at the shadows in the coulee . . .
And you, rolled warm among the beaver-pelts,
Forgetful of your Sickness-on-the-lung,
Of the fever-pains and coughs that racked your bones—
You, beating a war song on your drum,
And laughing as the scarlet-moccasined flames
Danced on the coals and billowed up the sky.

Don't you remember? . . . the snowflakes drifting down
Thick as the falling petals of wild plums . . .
The clinker-ice and the scudding fluff of the whirlpool
Muffling the summer-mumblings of the brook . . .
The turbulent waterfall protesting against
Such early winter-sleep, like a little boy
Who struggles with the calamity of slumber,
Knuckling his leaden lids and his tingling nose
With a pudgy fist, and fretfully flinging back
His snowy covers with his petulant fingers.
Out on the windy barrens restless bands
Of caribou, rumped up against the gale,
Suddenly breaking before the rabid blast,
Scampering off like tumbleweeds in a cyclone . . .
The low of bulls from the hills where worried moose,
Nibbling the willows, the wintergreens, the birches,
Were yarding up in the sheltering alder-thicket . . .
From the cedar wind-break, the bleat of fawns wedged warm
Against the bellies of their drowsy does . . .
And then the utter calm . . . the wide white drift
That lay upon the world as still and ghastly
As the winding-sheet of death . . . the sudden snap
Of a dry twig . . . the groan of sheeted rivers

Beating with naked hands upon the ice . . .
The brooding night . . . the crackle of cold skies . . .

"*Sh-sh-sh! . . . Look, my frien'—somebody's dere!*
Ain't? . . . over dere? He's come from Land-of-Winter!
Wit' quilt he's cover-um up dose baby mink,
Dose cub, dose wild arbutus, dose jump-up-Johnny . . .
He's keep hees chil'ens warm for long, long winter . . .
Sh-sh-sh! . . . Somebody's dere on de w'ite savanna!
Somebody's dere! . . . He's walk-um in de timber . . .
He's cover-um up hees chil'ens, soft . . . soft . . ."

And later, when your bird-claw fingers rippled
Over the holes of your cedar bée-bee-gwún
Mellowly in a tender tune, how the stars,
Like little children trooping from their teepees,
Danced with their nimble feet across the sky
To the running-water music of your flute . . .
And how, with twinkling heels they scurried off
Before the Northern Light swaying, twisting,
Spiralling like a slender silver smoke
On the thin blue winds, and feeling out among
The frightened starry children of the sky . . .

"*Look!—in de Land-of-Winter—somet'ing's dere!*
Somebody—he's reaching out hees hand!—for me!
Ain't? . . . For me he's waiting. Somebody's dere!
Somebody he's in dere, waiting . . . waiting . . ."

Don't you remember?—the ghostly silence, splintered
At last by a fist that cracked the hoary birch,

By a swift black fist that shattered the brittle air,
Splitting it into a million frosty fragments . . .
And dreary Northwind, coughing in the snow,
Spitting among the glistening sheeted pines,
And moaning on the barrens among the bones
Of gaunt white tamaracks mournful and forlorn . . .

> *"Sh-sh-sh-sh! . . . My Caribou! Somebody's dere!*
> *He's crying . . . little bit crazy in dose wind . . .*
> *Ain't? . . . You hear-um . . . far 'way . . . crying*
> *Lak my old woman w'en she's lose de baby*
> *And no can find-um—w'en she's running everyw'ere*
> *Falling in snow, talking little bit crazy,*
> *Calling and crying for shees little boy . . .*
> *Sh-sh-sh! . . . Somet'ing's dere—you hear-um? . . . ain't?*
> *Somebody—somebody's dere, crying . . . crying . . ."*

Then from the swale, where shadows pranced grotesquely
Solemn, like phantom puppets on a string,
A cry—pointed, brittle, perpendicular—
As startling as a thin stiff blade of ice
Laid swift and sharp on fever-burning flesh:
The tremulous wail of a lonely shivering wolf,
Piercing the world's great heart like an icy sword . . .

> *"Look! . . . Quick!—Ah-déek! . . . Somebody's dere!*
> *Ain't? . . . He's come—he's come for me—for me!*
> *Me—me, I go! . . . . My Caribou—*
> *Dose fire—dose fire she's going out—she's cold . . .*
> *T'row—t'row on dose knots of pine . . . Mee-gwétch!*
> *And pull 'way from dose flame—dose pan of sour-dough,*
> *If you want eat—in de morning—plenty good flapjack.*

73

"Sh-sh-sh-sh! Somet'ing's dere! . . . You hear-um? ain't?
Somebody—somebody's dere, calling . . . calling . . .
I go . . . . . I go—me! . . . . . me . . . . . I go. . . ."

III

TALKING WATERS

O eagle whose whistling wings have known the lift
Of high mysterious hands, and the wild sweet music
Of big winds among the ultimate stars,
The black-robes put you in a box of God,
Seeking in honest faith and holy zeal
To lay upon your lips new songs, to swell
The chorus of amens and hallelujahs.
O bundle of copper bones tossed in a hole,
Here in the place-of-death—God's-fenced-in-ground!—
Beneath these put-in-pines and waxen lilies,
They placed you in a crimson gash in the hillside,
Here on a bluff above the Sleepy-eye,
Where the Baptism River, mumbling among the canyons,
Shoulders its flood through crooning waterfalls
In a mist of wafted foam fragile as petals
Of windflowers blowing across the green of April;
Where ghosts of wistful leaves go floating up
In the rustling blaze of autumn, like silver smokes
Slenderly twisting among the thin blue winds;
Here in the great gray arms of Mont du Père,
Where the shy arbutus, the mink, and the Johnny-jump-up
Huddle and whisper of a long, long winter;
Where stars, with soundless feet, come trooping up
To dance to the water-drums of white cascades—

Where stars, like little children, go singing down
The sky to the flute of the wind in the willow-tree—
Somebody—somebody's there . . . O Pagan Joe . . .
Can't you see Him? as He moves among the mountains?
Where dusk, dew-lidded, slips among the valleys
Soft as a blue wolf walking in thick wet moss?
Look!—my friend!—at the breast of Mont du Père! . . .
Sh-sh-sh-sh! . . . Don't you hear His talking waters? . . .
Soft in the gloom as broken butterflies
Hovering above a somber pool . . . Sh-sh-sh-sh!
Somebody's there . . . in the heart of Mont du Père . . .
Somebody—somebody's there, sleeping . . . sleeping . . .

B – FLYING MOCCASINS

THE SQUAW-DANCE

Beat, beat, beat, beat, beat upon the tom-tom,
Beat, beat, beat, beat, beat upon the drum.
Hóy-eeeeeee-yáh! Hóy-eeeeeee-yáh!
Shuffle to the left, shuffle to the left,
Shuffle, shuffle, shuffle to the left, to the left.
Fat squaws, lean squaws, gliding in a row,
Grunting, wheezing, laughing as they go;
Bouncing up with a scuffle and a twirl,
Flouncing petticoat and hair in a whirl.
Rheumatic hags of gristle and brawn,
Rolling in like a ponderous billow;
Fair squaws lithe as the leaping fawn,
Swaying with the wind and bending with the willow;
Bouncing buttock and shriveled shank,
Scuffling to the drumbeat, rank on rank;
Stolid eye and laughing lip,
Buxom bosom and jiggling hip,
Weaving in and weaving out,
Hí! Hí! Hí! with a laugh and a shout,
To the beat, beat, beat, beat, beat upon the tom-tom,
Beat, beat, beat, beat, beat upon the drum;
Hóy-eeeeeee-yáh! Hóy-eeeeeee-yáh!
Hí! Hí! Hí! Hí! Hóy-eeeeeeeeeeeeee-yáh!

Medicine-men on the medicine-drum,
Beating out the rhythm—here they come!
Medicine-gourd with its rattle, rattle, rattle,

76

Flinging wild with the call of battle.
Beaded drummers squatting in the ring
Leap to its challenge with a crouch and a spring;
Weathered old bucks who grunt and wheeze
As they jangle bells on their wrists and their knees:
Shining new and olden bells,
Silver, copper, golden bells,
Cow-bells, toy bells, ringing sleigh-bells,
Beaded dance bells, "give-away" bells,
Jingling, jangling, jingling bells,
Set-the-toes-atingling bells—
To the beat, beat, beat, beat, beat upon the tom-tom,
Beat, beat, beat, beat, beat upon the drum;
Hóy-eeeeeee-yáh! Hóy-eeeeeee-yáh!
Hí! Hi! Hí! Hi! Hóy-eeeeeeeeeeeeee-yáh!

Old bucks stamping heel and toe,
Ugh! as they snort and they cackle and they crow;
Yowling like the lynx that crouches nigh,
Howling like the wolf at the prairie sky;
Growling and grunting as they shift and they tramp,
Stalking, crouching—with a stamp, stamp, stamp—
Sleek limbs, lithe limbs, strong and clean limbs,
Withered limbs, bowed limbs, long and lean limbs;
Flat feet, bare feet, dancing feet,
Buckskin-moccasined prancing feet,
Eager child-feet, scuffling feet,
Feet, feet, feet, feet, shuffling feet!
Hi! Beat, beat, beat, beat, beat upon the tom-tom,
Beat, beat, beat, beat, beat upon the drum;
Shuffle to the left, shuffle to the left,

Shuffle, shuffle, shuffle to the left, to the left—
Hí! Hi! Hí! Hi! Hóy-eeeeeeeeeeeeee-yáh!

KEE-WÁY-DIN-Ó-KWAY, THE "NORTH-WIND-WOMAN,"
SPEAKS WHEN THE DANCE CEASES FOR A MINUTE:

"I have a pretty present for Mah-éen-gans,
For 'Little-Wolf' I have a pretty medicine-bag.
Broidered upon it are many little beads
In many pretty patterns of wild lilies—
Yellow beads and beads of the color of the cornflower.
Through the many winter moons
I labored on this gift of friendship;
In this gaily patterned medicine-bag
I left my weary eyes and my worn fingers.
Now I wish 'the Wolf' to dance with me in the ring.
Hi! Beat, beat upon the drums, old medicine-men!
Dance! Dance in the ring, my people, and sing!"

Ho! Hó! Ho! Hó!
Hi-yáh! Hi-yáh!

Hóy-eeeeeeeee-yáh! Hóy-eeeeeeeee-yáh!
Hí! Hi! Hí! Hi! Hóy-eeeeeeeeeee-yáh!
Beat, beat, beat, beat, beat upon the tom-tom,
Beat, beat, beat, beat, beat upon the drum,
As a bouncing breast and a lean long thigh,
Caper to the ring with a whoop and a cry,
And shuffle to the left, shuffle to the left,
Shuffle, shuffle, shuffle to the left, to the left—
Hí! Hi! Hí! Hi! Hóy-eeeeeeeeee-yáh!

78

"I have a present for the 'Wind-Woman,'
A present equal in value to her medicine-bag.
Ho! A pretty present, a mí-gis chain
Of many little mí-gis shells—
As beautiful as the 'North-Wind-Woman.'
My chain of shells will shake
And shimmer on her breast
As the silver brooks that tinkle
Down the moonlit bosom of yonder mountain.
Now I wish the woman to dance with me in the ring.
Hi! Beat, beat upon the drums, old medicine-men!
Dance! Dance in the ring, my people, and sing!"

Ho! Hó! Ho! Hó!
Hi-yáh! Hi-yáh!

Hóy-eeeeeeeeeeee-yáh! Hóy-eeeeeeeeeeee-yáh!
Hí! Hi! Hí! Hi! Hóy-eeeeeeeeeeeeeeeee-yáh!
Beat, beat, beat, beat, beat upon the tom-tom,
Beat, beat, beat, beat, beat upon the drum.
Medicine-gourd with its rattle, rattle, rattle,
Ringing wild with the call of battle.
Rheumatic hags of gristle and brawn,
Rolling in like a ponderous billow;
Fair squaws lithe as the leaping fawn,
Swaying with the wind and bending with the willow.
Bouncing buttock and shriveled shank,
Scuffling to the drumbeat, rank on rank.
Old bucks stamping heel and toe,

Ugh! as they snort and they cackle and they crow—
Sleek limbs, lithe limbs, strong and clean limbs,
Withered limbs, bowed limbs, long and lean limbs;
Flat feet, bare feet, dancing feet,
Buckskin-moccasined prancing feet;
Shuffle to the left, shuffle to the left,
Shuffle, shuffle, shuffle to the left, to the left;
With a crouch and a spring and a grunt and a wheeze,
And a clanging of bells at the wrists and the knees:
Shining new and olden bells,
Silver, copper, golden bells—
Feet, feet, feet, feet, scuffling feet!
To the drumbeat, drumbeat, beat, beat, beat—
Hí! Hi! Hí! Hi! Hóy-eeeeeeeee-yáh!

THE BLUE DUCK

Hí! Hi! Hí! Hi!
Hí! Hi! Hí! Hi!
Kéetch-ie Má-ni-dó, Má-ni-dó,
The hunter-moon is chipping,
Chipping at his flints,
At his dripping bloody flints.
He is rising for the hunt,
And his face is red with blood
From the spears of many spruces,
And his blood is on the leaves
That flutter down.
The Winter-Maker, white Bee-bóan,
Is walking in the sky,
And his windy blanket
Rustles in the trees.
He is blazing out the trail
Through the fields of nodding rice
For the swift and whistling wings
Of his She-shé-be,
For the worn and weary wings
Of many duck—
Ho! Plenty duck! Plenty duck!
Ho! Plenty, plenty duck!

Hí! Hi! Hí! Hi!
Hí! Hi! Hí! Hi!
Kéetch-ie Má-ni-dó, Má-ni-dó,

The seasons have been barren.
In the Moon-of-Sugar-Making,
And the Moon-of-Flowers-and-Grass,
From the blighted berry patches
And the maple-sugar bush,
The hands of all my children
Came home empty, came home clean.
The big rain of Nee-bín, the Summer-Maker,
Washed away the many little partridge.
And good Ad-ík-kum-áig, sweet whitefish,
Went sulking all the summer-moons,
Hiding in the deepest waters,
Silver belly in the mud,
And he would not walk into my nets! Ugh!
Thus the skin-sacks and the mó-kuks
Hang within my wéeg-i-wam empty.

Soon the winter moon will come,
Slipping through the silent timber,
Walking on the silent snow,
Stalking on the frozen lake.
Lean-bellied,
Squatting with his rump upon the ice,
The phantom wolf will fling
His wailings to the stars.
Then Wéen-di-gó, the Devil-Spirit,
Whining through the lodge-poles,
Will clutch and shake my teepee,
Calling,
Calling,
Calling as he sifts into my lodge;

And ghostly little shadow-arms
Will float out through
The smoke-hole in the night—
Leaping, tossing shadow-arms,
Little arms of little children,
Hungry hands of shadow-arms,
Clutching,
Clutching,
Clutching at the breast that is not there . . .
Shadow-arms and shadow breasts . . .
Twisting,
Twisting,
Twisting in and twisting out
On the ghostly clouds of smoke . . .
Riding on the whistling wind . . .
Riding on the whistling wind . . .
Riding on the whistling wind . . .
Starward! . . .
Blow, blow, blow Kee-wáy-din, North Wind,
Warm and gentle on my children,
Cold and swift upon the wild She-shé-be,
Ha-a-ah-ee-ooo! . . . Plenty duck . . .
Ha-a-a-a-ah-eeee-ooooo! . . . Plenty duck. . . .

Hí! Hi! Hí! Hi!
Hí! Hi! Hí! Hi!
Kéetch-ie Má-ni-dó, Má-ni-dó,
Blow on Áh-bi-tóo-bi many wings;
Wings of teal and wings of mallard,
Wings of green and blue.
My little lake lies waiting,

Singing for her blustery lover;
Dancing on the golden-stranded shore
With many little moccasins,
Pretty little moccasins,
Beaded with her silver sands,
And with her golden pebbles.
And upon her gentle bosom
Lies mah-nó-min, sweetest wild rice,
Green and yellow,
Rustling blade and rippling blossom—
Hi-yee! Hi-yee! Blow on Áh-bi-tóo-bi plenty duck!
Ho! Plenty, plenty duck!
Ho! Plenty duck, plenty duck!
Ho! Ho!

Hí! Hi! Hí! Hi!
Hí! Hi! Hí! Hi!
Kéetch-ie Má-ni-dó, Má-ni-dó,
I place this pretty duck upon your hand;
Upon its sunny palm and in its windy fingers.
Hi-yeee! Blue and beautiful
Is he, beautifully blue!
Carved from sleeping cedar
When the stars like silver fishes
Were aquiver in the rivers of the sky;
Carved from dripping cedar
When the Kóo-koo-kóo dashed hooting
At the furtive feet
That rustle in the leaves—
Hi! And seasoned many moons, many moons,
Ho! Seasoned many, many, many sleeps!

Hi-yeee! Blue and beautiful
Is he, beautifully blue!
Though his throat is choked with wood,
And he honks not on his pole,
And his wings are weak with hunger,
Yet his heart is plenty good.
Hi-yee! His heart is plenty good!
Hi-yee! Plenty good, plenty good!
Hi-yee! Hi-yee! Hi-yee! His heart is good!

My heart like his is good!

Ugh! My tongue talks straight!

Ho!

THUNDERDRUMS

I

THE DRUMMERS SING:

Beat on the buckskin, beat on the drums,
Hí! Hi! Hí! for the Thunderbird comes;
His eyes burn red with the blood of battle;
His wild wings roar in the medicine-rattle.
Thunderbird-god, while our spirits dance,
Tip with your lightning the warrior's lance;
On shafts of wind, with heads of flame,
Build for us arrows that torture and maim;
Ho! may our ironwood war-clubs crash
With a thunderbolt head and a lightning flash.
Hí! Hi! Hí! hear the Cut-throat's doom,
As our wild bells ring and our thunderdrums boom.

II

DOUBLE-BEAR DANCES

Hí! Hi! Hí
My wild feet fly,
For I follow the track
Of a cowardly pack;
Footprints here,
Footprints there—
Enemies near!—
Taint in the air!
Signs on the sod!
Ho! the Thunderbird-god

Gives me the eye
Of a hawk in the sky!—
Beat, beat on the drums,
For the Thunderbird comes.

Ho! Ho!
Ho! Ho!

III

BIG-SKY DANCES

Ho! hear me shout—
A Pucker-skin scout
With a nose that is keen
For winds unclean.
Look! Look! Look!
At the distant nook,
Where the hill-winds drift
As the night-fogs lift:
Ten smokes I see
Of the Cut-throat Sioux—
Ten ghosts there will be—
Ten plumes on my coup;
For my arms grow strong
With my medicine-song,
And a Pucker-skin scout
Has a heart that is stout.
Beat, beat on the drums,
For the Thunderbird comes.

Háh-yah-ah-háy!
Háh-yah-ah-háy!

IV

GHOST-WOLF DANCES

Hó! Ho! Hó!
In the winds that blow
From yonder hill,
When the night is still,
What do I hear
With my Thunderbird ear?
Down from the river
A gray wolf's wail?
Coyotes that shiver
And slink the tail?
Ugh! enemies dying—
And women crying!—
For Cut-throat men—
One, two . . . nine, ten.
Hó! Ho! Hó!
The Spirit-winds blow—
Beat, beat on the drums,
For the Thunderbird comes.

Ah-hah-háy!
Ah-hah-háy!

V

IRON-WIND DANCES

Over and under
The shaking sky,
The war-drums thunder

88

When I dance by!
Ho! a warrior proud,
I dance on a cloud,
For my ax shall feel
The enemy reel;
My heart shall thrill
To a bloody kill—
Ten Sioux dead
Split open of head!
Look! to the West!—
The sky-line drips—
Blood from the breast!
Blood from the lips!
Ho! when I dance by,
The war-drums thunder
Over and under
The shaking sky.
Beat, beat on the drums,
For the Thunderbird comes.

Wuh!
Wuh!

VI

THE DRUMMERS SING:

Beat on the buckskin, beat on the drums,
Hí! Hí! Hí! for the Thunderbird comes;
His eyes glow red with the lust for battle,
And his wild wings roar in the medicine-rattle.
Thunderbird-god, while our spirits dance,

Tip with your lightning the warrior's lance;
On shafts of wind, with heads of flame,
Build for us arrows that torture and maim;
Ho! may our ironwood war-clubs crash
With a thunderbolt head and a lightning flash.
Hí! Hi! Hí! hear the Cut-throat's doom,
As our wild bells ring and our thunderdrums boom.

C – TAMARACK BLUE

As any brush-wolf, driven from the hills
By winter famine, waits upon the fringe
Of a settlement for cover of the dusk,
And enters it by a furtive, devious route,
Cowering among the shadows, freezing taut
With every sound—so came the widow Blue
In winter-moons to parish Pointe aux Trembles,
Doubled to earth beneath her pack of furs,
To ply her trade, to barter at the Post.
And if she ventured near the village inn,
Baring their yellow tusks the roustabouts
Would toss a dry slow leer at her and stone
Old Tamarack numb with "Mag, the Indian hag,"
With ribald epithet and jibe and gesture.
And when they waxed melodious with rum,
Pounding their ribs, and knew no way to free
The head of steam that hammered in their breasts,
Save in a raucous music, they would blare:
"She wears for a petticoat a gunny bag"—
Adding, with many ponderous knowing winks,
"Oh, Skinflint Blue, with a shin of flint, too";
And thus to the end they thumped their maudlin song
With laughter raw, big-bellied. There were days
When the Christian gentlemen of Pointe aux Trembles
Would welcome Tamarack with such fusillade
Of bilious humor that the harried squaw,
Bruised by their epithets, with swimming eyes
Intent upon the dust, seemed well-nigh gone,
Stoned to the earth; there came a stumbling hour

When I put an arm around her bag of ribs,
And felt her bosom pounding with such fear
That had I dared to place my weight of thumb
Upon her heart, I could have pressed the life
From her as from a fluttering crippled wren
Held in my hand.

               Nor was the widow's perfume
Of name and reputation without reason:
Penurious, forgetful of her own
Hungering flesh, she strangled every coin
And hoarded it against some secret need;
And slattern she was—a juiceless crone, more drab
To contemplate than venison long-cured
By the slow smoke of burning maple logs—
And quite as pungent with the wilderness.
What with the fight to draw the sap of life
From grudging toil, in sun and wind and snow,
Twenty-one years of Indian widowhood
Will parch a soul and weather any hide
To the texture of a withered russet apple:
A moon of hauling sap in the sugar-bush,
Of boiling maple-syrup; a moon for netting
Whitefish and smoking them upon the racks;
Two moons among the berries, plums, and cherries;
A moon in the cranberry bog; another moon
For harvesting the wild rice in the ponds;
Odd days for trailing moose and jerking meat;
And then the snow—and trap-lines to be strung
Among the hills for twenty swampy miles,
For minks and martens, otters, beavers, wolves.

So steadfast was the bronzed coureuse de bois
On her yearly round—like hands upon a clock—
Given the week and weather, I could tell
As surely as the needle of a compass
Finds the magnetic pole, what grove of spruce,
What jutting rock or lonely waste of swamp
Sheltered the widow's bones at night from beat
Of rain or snow.

              And when the spring thaws came,
And bread was low, and her pagan stomach lay
As flat against her spine as any trout's
After a spawning-season, there were nights
When Tamarack's ears were sensitive to silver—
Evenings when any lumberjack on drive,
Gone rampant with the solitude of winter
And hungry for affection, might persuade
The otherwise forlorn and famished widow
To join him in a moment of romance.
Oh, not without demurring did she yield—
And not without reason: otter pelts are rare,
Cranberries buy no silken petticoats,
No singing lessons—for there was Susie Blue.

Whenever Tamarack touched the world in shame
Or drudgery or barter, she had for end
The wringing of a comfort for her daughter—
As when a cactus pushes down its roots
Among the hostile sands for food and moisture,
And sends the stream and sparkle of its life
Up to a creaming blossom. None of us

In parish Pointe aux Trembles could fathom why
The outcast crucified herself for Susie.
Some said that Susie Blue was all the kin
The starveling had; and others, among the elders,
Held that the half-breed daughter carried every
Feature of Antoine Blue, who fathered her,
As clearly as a tranquil mountain-pool
Holds on its breast the overhanging sky;
And added that the pagan drab was proud
That she had crossed to the issue of her flesh
The pure white strain, the color of a Frenchman.
Whatever the reason, when the voyageur
Let out his quart of blood upon the floor
After a drunken brawl at Jock McKay's,
The widow set herself to live for Susie,
Bustling from crimson dawn to purple dusk—
And sometimes in the furtive black of night—
Hither and yon, in every wind and weather,
Scratching the mulch for morsels of the earth,
And salvaging the tender bits—a grouse
With a solitary chick. Of luxuries
Wrung from the widow's frame there was no end:
Ribbons and scarves and laces—all for Susie;
And four long years at Indian boarding-school;
A year at Fort de Bois in business-college
For higher education; and, topping all,
Three seasons spent in culture of the voice.
Oh, such a dream as stirred the widow's heart!—
A hope that put a savor in her world,
A zest for life; a dream of cities thralled
By silver music fountaining from Susie,

Cities that flashed upon the velvet night
In scrawling fire the name of Susie Blue;
A dream wherein the widow would declare
In glory, comfort, rest, her dividends
Upon the flesh put in for capital.

How clearly I recall the eventful spring
When Sue returned from her gilding at the Fort!
Old Tamarack was away—at Lac la Croix
Netting for fish—and could not come to town
To welcome her. But when the run of trout
Was at an end, she cached her nets and floats
And paddled down in time for Corpus Christi.
Some circumstance conspired to keep the two
Apart until the eucharistic feast—
Perhaps the village folk who always took
A Christian interest in Susie's morals.
But Thursday found the wistful derelict
Stiff on a bench in Mission Sacré Coeur
More taut for the high sweet moment of her life
Than quivering catgut strung upon a fiddle—
For Susie was to sing in Corpus Christi;
The pagan was about to claim her own.

I'd never seen the squaw in her Sunday-best:
Soft doeskin moccasins of corn-flower blue,
Patterned with lemon beads and lemon quills;
Checkered vermilion gown of calico
To hide her flinty shins, her thin flat hips;
An umber shawl, drawn tight about her head
And anchored at her breast by leather hands—

A dubious madonna of the pines.
Somehow the crone had burst her dull cocoon
Upon this day, was almost radiant
With loveliness, as if upon the new-born
Wings of desire she were about to leave
The earth and know the luxury of sunlight.
The apologetic eyes, the mien of one
Bludgeoned to earth by rancid drollery,
Had vanished; on her face there was the look
That glorifies a partridge once in life—
When, after endless labor, pain, and trouble
Rearing her first-born brood, she contemplates
Her young ones pattering among the leaves
On steady legs, and, clucking pridefully,
Outspreads her shining feathers to the wind.
And when the widow shot a wisp of smile
At me from underneath her umber cowl—
A smile so tremulous, so fragmentary,
And yet so shyly confident that all
The dawning world this day was exquisite,
A whisk of overture so diffident
And yet so palpitant for friendliness—
Somehow the poignant silver of it slipped
Between my ribs and touched me at the quick,
And I was moved to join her in her pew.

Oh, how her eyes, like embers in a breeze,
Flared up to life when Father Bruno led
Her daughter from the choir and Susie set
Herself to sing. Susie was beautiful,
Sullenly beautiful with sagging color:

Blue was the half-seen valley of her breast;
Her blue hair held the dusk; beneath her lids
Blue were the cryptic shadows, stealthy blue,
Skulking with wraiths that spoke of intimate,
Too intimate, communion with the night,
The languor of the moon. Beneath the glass
Of hothouse culture she had come to fruit,
A dusky grape grown redolent with wine,
A grape whose velvet-silver bloom reveals
The finger-smudge of too many dawdling thumbs.

She braced herself and tossed a cataract
Of treble notes among the mission rafters,
While Sister Mercy followed on the organ.
Something distressed me in the melody—
A hint of metal, a subtle dissonance;
Perhaps the trouble lay with Sister Mercy,
Or else the organ needful of repair.
To me there seemed a mellow spirit wanting,
As if the chambers of the half-breed's soul—
Like a fiddle-box, unseasoned by the long
Slow sun and wind, and weathered too rapidly
Beside a comfortable hothouse flame—
Lacked in the power to resonate the tone.
But the widow sat beatified, enthralled;
To her the cold flat notes were dulcet-clear,
As golden in their tones as the slow bronze bell
That swung among the girders overhead
And echoed in the hills. And Susie sang,
Serene, oblivious of all the world—
Save in a dim far pew a florid white man

Whose glance went up her bosom to her lips
And inventoried all of Susie's charms.
Was it for him she chanted? lifted up
The tawny blue-veined marble of her arm
In a casual gesture to pat a random lock?
For him she shook her perfume on the air?—
Bold as a young deer rutting in October,
Drenching its heavy musk upon the wind,
And waiting—silhouetted on the moon—
Waiting the beat of coming cloven hoofs.

When Sue dispatched her final vibrant note
In a lingering amen and came to earth,
She undulated down the aisle with a swash
Of silken petticoat to greet and join
Her glorified old mother—so it seemed.
And when she came within the pagan's reach,
The widow, bright with tears, and tremulous,
Uttered a rivulet of ecstasy
As wistful as the wind in autumn boughs,
And strove to touch the hand of Sue, half stood
To welcome her. The daughter paused, uncertain,
The passing of a breath. Haunted her face;
The dear dim ghosts of wildwood yesterdays
Laid gentle hands upon the half-breed's heart,
Struggled to bring her soul to life again.
She wavered. Then conscious of the battery
Of parish eyes on her, the village code
Rich with taboos of blue and flinty flesh,
And mindful of the gulf between the two,
Sprung from her Christian culture at the Fort,

She gathered up her new-born pride, and froze.
With eyes as cold and stony as a pike's
She looked at Tamarack—as on a vagrant wind;
With but the tremor of a lip, a fleeting
Hail and farewell, she slipped her flaccid palm
From out the pagan's gnarled and weathered hand
And rustled down the room and out the door,
The stranger at her heels—a coyote warm
And drooling on the trail of musky deer.

The widow held her posture, breathless, stunned;
Swayed for a moment, blindly groped her way,
And wilted to the bench—as when a mallard,
High on a lift of buoyant homing wind,
Before a blast of whistling lead, careers,
Hovers bewildered, and, crumpling up its wings,
Plummets to earth, to lie upon the dust
A bleeding thing, suffused with anguish, broken.
At last she gathered the remnants of her strength;
Huddling within her corner, stoic, cold,
And burying her head within her cowl,
She parried all the gimlet eyes that strove
To penetrate the shadows to her mood.
And when the curé lifted up his hands
And blessed his flock, the derelict went shuffling
Along the aisle and vanished in the mist
Of Lac la Croix.

                    Some untoward circumstance
Stifled my breath—perhaps the atmosphere,
The fetid body-odors in the room.

I hurried from the hall to sun-washed air.
Bridling my sorrel mare, I found the trail
That skirts the mossy banks of Stonybrook,
And cantered homeward to all the kindred-folk
That ever wait my coming with high heart:
My setter bitch asprawl beside the door,
Drowsy, at peace with all the droning flies;
The woodchucks, quizzical and palpitant,
That venture from their den among the logs
To query me for crumbs; the crippled doe,
Who, lodging with me, crops my meadow-grass
And tramples havoc in my bed of beets,
Gloriously confident that I shall never
Muster the will to serve her with a notice—
To all that blessed wildwood company
With whom I band myself against the world
And all its high concerns and tribulations.

Somehow the valley was uncommonly
Serene and lovely, following the rain,
The mellow benediction of the sun.
The beaver-ponds that held upon their glass
The clean clear blue of noon, the pebbly brook
Meandering its twisted silver rope
Through hemlock arches, loitering in pools
Clear-hued as brimming morning-glories, placid,
Save when a trout would put a slow round kiss
Upon the water—these were beautiful.
The rustle of winds among the aspen-trees,
The fragrance on the air when my sorrel mount,
Loping upon the trail, flung down her hoofs

Upon the wintergreen and left it bruised
And dripping—these were very clean and cool.
And I was glad for the wild plums crimsoning
Among the leaves, and for the frail blue millers
Glinting above them—chips of a splintered sky;
Glad for the blossoming alfalfa fields
Robust with wining sap, and the asters bobbing
And chuckling at the whimsies of the breeze;
Glad for the far jang-jangling cattle-bells
That intimated a land of deep wet grass
And lazy water, a world of no distress,
No pain, no sorrow, a valley of contentment.

Until I came upon a mullein stalk,
Withered and bended almost to the ground
Beneath the weight of a raucous purple grackle—
A weed so scrawny of twig, so gnarled, so old,
That when I flung a pebble at the bird
Heavy upon the bough, and the purple bird
Soared singing into heaven, the mullein failed
To spring its ragged blades from earth again—
The suppleness of life had gone from it.
Something in this distressed me, haunted me.
Something in mullein, stricken, drooping, doomed—
When I can hear the rustle of a ghost
Upon November wind, a ghost that whispers
Of chill white nights and brittle stars to come,
Of solitude with never a creature sounding,
Save lowing moose, bewildered by the snow,
Forlornly rumped against the howling wind—
Something in palsied mullein troubles me.

CLIFF-DWELLERS

Out of this canyon-depth bronze women clambered,
Juggling their jars of water; on this rock
That juts above the gorge they ground their maize;
Deep in this cavern—now tenement of bats
And shifty centipedes—from wide strong loins
They stoically dropped their young on buffalo-robes
Suckled their babes to strength, and fell away
At last to querulous bags of bone and parchment.

Leaping like mountain-goats among these crags,
Children, as wild as kids, as nimble-toed,
Naked and round and marble-hard of belly,
Went catapulting legs and arms in play,
Gambled with death upon this canyon-rim,
And filled the elders' eyes with pride and fear.

Upon this cedar-cloistered shelf of granite,
When twilight draped its veils of heliotrope
Over the desert-gold, and night was cool
With the breath of junipers and pines,
Bronze lovers rippled their supple muscles,
And cradled themselves upon the sleek brown limbs
Of women through long-drawn starry nights,
Untroubled by the mourn of desert-wolves.

The tough flat feet of dancing bucks once shook
The earth of this expanse of web-hung kiva;
Gaunt shamen thundered on their drums,
Rattled their gourds and spread medicine-bundles
To put the evil spirits into flight,
To conjure arrowy clouds across the blue
And rain for the parched and panting desert's mouth.

Here on this mesa-citadel that looms
Above the shimmering vermilion waste
Of sand and cactus, of sun-baked water-hole,
Old men with shrewd slow tongues and squinting eyes
Squatted upon the brink of the precipice,
Maintained their watch upon the valley-trails,
And mumbled together of their yesterdays.

Tonight the moon will flood its silver foam
Over the cliffs and with a lean pale hand
Call up from these dark caves a hundred ghosts—
Patriarchs, children, warriors, lovers, priests,
Haulers of jars of water, grinders of corn,
Molders of silver and polishers of turquoise.

Deep in arroyo-gloom the prowling wolf
Will stretch his gullet and toss ironic laughter
Into the starry caverns of the sky.

INDIAN LOVE SONG

Cold sky and frozen star
That look upon me from afar
  Know my echoed grief.

Hollow night and black butte
Hear my melancholy flute—
  Oh, sound of falling leaf.

Homeless wind and waterfall
Hold a sadness in their call,
  A sorrow I have known.

Shivering wolf and lonely loon
Cry my sorrow to the moon—
  O heavy heart . . . O stone!

INDIAN SLEEP SONG

Zhóo . . . zhoo, zhóo!
My little brown chief,
The bough of the willow
Is rocking the leaf;
The sleepy wind cries
To you, close your eyes—
O little brown chief,
Zhóo . . . zhoo, zhóo!

Kóo . . . . koo, kóo!
My little brown bird,
A wood-dove was dreaming
And suddenly stirred;
A brown mother-dove,
Dreaming of love—
O little brown bird,
Kóo . . . . koo, kóo!

Hóo . . . . hoo, hóo!
My little brown owl,
Yellow-eye frightens
Bad spirits that prowl;
For you she will keep
A watch while you sleep—
O little brown owl,
Hóo . . . . hoo, hóo!

Zhóo . . . zhoo, zhóo!
O leaf in the breeze.

Kóo . . . . koo, kóo!
Shy bird in the trees.
Sh . . . . . . sh, sh!
O snow-covered fawn.
Hóo . . . . hoo, hóo!
Sleep softly till dawn.

CRAZY-MEDICINE

Blow winds, winds blow,
North, East, South, West,
Make my foe, the cedar man,
Drunk with crazy dances;
Shake his skull until his brains
Rattle up and rattle down—
Pebbles in a gourd.

Roar winds, winds roar,
Flapping winds, jumping winds,
Winds that crush and winds that split,
Winds like copper lances;
Whistle through the crazy man,
Fling him up, fling him down—
A rag upon a cord.

Beat winds, winds beat,
Iron winds, icy winds,
Winds with hail like leaden shot
That make a sounding thunder;
Beat a sleet upon his head,
Up and down, up and down—
Hail upon a drum.

Wail winds, winds wail,
Silver winds, pointed winds,
Winds to stab a coyote soul,
In and out and under;
Send cold silver through his head,
In an ear, out an ear—
A needle through a plum.

BEAT AGAINST ME NO LONGER

Ai-yee! My Yellow-Bird-Woman,
My né-ne-móosh-ay, ai-yee! my Loved-One,
Be not afraid of my eyes!
Beat against me no longer!
Come! Come with a yielding of limbs!
Ai-yee! Woman, woman,
Trembling there in the teepee
Like the doe in the season of mating,
Why foolishly fearest thou me?
Cast the strange doubts from thy bosom!
Be not afraid of my eyes!
Be not as the flat-breasted squaw-sich
Who feels the first womanly yearnings
And hides, by the law of our people,
Alone three sleeps in the forest;
Be not as that brooding young woman
Who wanders forlorn in the cedars,
And slumbers with troubled dreams,
To awaken suddenly, fearing
The hot throbbing blood in her bosom,
The strange eager life in her limbs.
Ai-yee! Foolish one, woman,
Cast the strange fears from thy heart!
Wash the red shame from thy face!
Be not afraid of my glances!

Be as the young silver birch
In the Moon-of-the-Green-Growing-Flowers—
Who sings with the thrill of the sap

As it leaps to the south wind's caresses;
Who yields her rain-swollen buds
To the kiss of the sun with glad dancing.
Be as the cool tranquil moon
Who flings off her silver-blue blanket
To bare her white breast to the pine;
Who walks through the many-eyed night
In her gleaming white nudeness
With proud eyes that will not look down.
Be as the sun in her glory,
Who dances across the blue day,
And flings her red soul, fierce-burning,
Into the arms of the twilight.
Ai-yee! Foolish one, woman,
Be as the sun and the moon!
Cast the strange doubts from thy bosom!
Wash the red shame from thy face!
Thou art a woman, a woman!
Beat against me no longer!
Be not afraid of my eyes!

E – COUNCIL FIRES

THE WINDS OF FIFTY WINTERS

The Weasel-Eye, the hawk-nosed one,
With the long white beard and soft white hands,
Arose before the Pillagers and Ottertails
Who squatted by the council-fire.
Fixing on his nose the little windows,
And putting on his face a pretty smile,
The Weasel-Eye "made talk, big talk":

THE WEASEL-EYE TALKS:

"My brothers, good red brothers,
Brothers each and all,
By me, his honest trusted agent
Whose heart is good to the Indian,
The Great White Chief sends greetings
To his good red children—
Ah! and many pretty presents!"

Ho!
Hi-yáh! Hi-yáh!
How! How! How!
Wuh!

"Gaze ye!—Flashing silver-glass
And tinkling copper bells!
And powder kegs and beads,
And tall black shining hats!

Ye shall walk arrayed
Like yon gorgeous blazing sun
If ye but heed my counsel."

Ho! Ho! Ho!

"Go ye North!
Forsake these rolling hills,
This vast, this too-vast country.
Forsake these wolf-infested forests,
That Pale-Face tillers of the soil
May lay their Iron-Roads
And scratch the ground for harvests.
Go ye North! to the barren lands,
To the land of the marked-out ground.
And though there be no moose
Within its flame-swept timber,
Nor whitefish in its waters,
Nor patches of wild berries,
Nor fields of nodding rice,
Yet will ye be content
For I shall pay ye well:
To every warrior, guns—
Six beavers' worth;
To every headman, blankets—
Red as yonder sky;
To every chieftain, ponies—
Six, more or less.
And there, in the marked-out North,
Your tribe may eat and dance
Forever and forever.

"Gaze upon me, O my brothers,
My good red brothers,
And heed ye well my counsel!
The winds of fifty winters
Have blown about my head,
And, lo! my hair is white with snow!
The winds of fifty winters
Have blown about my head,
And, lo! much wisdom lodged therein!
And from the winds of fifty winters,
Their wisdom, storms, and snows,
Lo! I counsel ye:
Sign ye this treaty!
Take ye the presents!
Go ye to the North!"

In the council-grove long silence fell,
But for a little laughing wind
That wandered in the pines.
Then, sinuous and supple as the wildcat,
Áh-nah-mah-keé, the "Thunderbolt," strode forward.
He stood a moment silent—
Straight as the Norway pine
That rears its head above the timber;
And in his eyes the many little lightnings flashed,
But on the corner of his mouth a sunbeam played:

THUNDERBOLT TALKS:

"O my brothers, my red brothers,
Brothers each and all,

112

The Weasel-Eye has spoken.
He has opened up his honey mouth;
And from the heart that is so good
He has poured his sounding words.
His heap-much pretty talk
Is like the tinkling stream
Of babbling sweet-water that gurgles
Down from the mountain springs;
But like the sweet-water of the brook,
That stops its pretty running
In the swamp and stands one sleep
In the deep and quiet pools,
The pretty words turn bitter-sour.

"Gaze upon me, O my brothers,
My good red brothers!
The winds of fifty winters
Have blown about my head,
And, lo! my hair is white with snow!
The winds of fifty winters
Have blown about my head,
And, lo! much wisdom lodged therein!
The winds of fifty winters
Have blown about my head—
But, lo! They have not blown away my brains!

"I am done!"

> *Ho!*
> *Hi! Hi!*
> *How! How! How!*

MEDALS AND HOLES

Boo-zhóo nee-chée! Me—Yellow-Otter,
I'm going mak'-um big-talk, 'Spector Jone'.

Look-see!—on chest I'm got-um golden medal;
Got-um woman on medal. Ho!—good medal!

Me—I'm go to Washin'ton long tam' ago;
Me—I'm tell-um Kéetch-ie Ó-gi-má, dose Big W'ite Chief:
"Eenzhuns no lak-um Eenzhun rese'vation;
No good! She's too much jack-pine, sand, and swamp."
Big-chief, him say: "Ó-zah-wah-kíg, you be good boy!
Go back to rese'vation. You tell-um tribe
If Eenzhun stay on rese'vation, Washin'ton gov'ment
Give-um all de Eenzhuns plenty payments, every year;
Give-um plenty good hats and suits o' clothes.
My heart is good to you; you damned good Eenzhun.
Me—I'm stick-um dis golden medal on your chest."
Ho! I'm walk-um home. I got-um medal—look-see!

But—me—no got-um plenty good hats and clothes;
No got-um every year; only every two year.
Clothes no good! Look-see! Got-um clothes on now—
No good! Got-um holes in legs—plenty-big holes
Wit' not much clot' around; and too much buttons off.
Gov'ment clothes she's coming every two year—
Long tam' between, too much—wit' too much holes.

Before de w'ite man come across Big-Water,
In olden tam', de Eenzhun got-um plenty clothes;

He mak'-um plenty suits wit' skins—no holes.
Even Shing-óos, dose weasel, and dose snowshoe rabbit,
Dey got-um better luck—two suits every year—
Summer, brown-yellow suit; winter, w'ite suit—
No got-um holes.
Wau-góosh and Nee-gíg, dose fox and otter,
Shang-wáy-she, dose mink, Ah-méek, dose beaver,
Dey get-um plenty clothes, each year two suits—
Summer, t'in clothes; winter, t'ick fur clothes—
No got-um holes.
Wásh-kish, dose big buck deer, and moose,
Each year dey t'row away deir horns;
In summer dey get-um nice new hat—
No got-um holes.
Me—I'm big-smart man, smarter dan weasel,
Smarter dan moose and fox and beaver;
Me—I'm also smart Eenzhun;
I got-um golden medal on chest from Big-Knife Chief;
But me—I'm only got-um one suit clothes
In two year—no-good clothes, no-good hats!
'Spector Jone', you tell-um our Big-Knife Preshident so:
"Yellow-Otter no got-um plenty good clothes;
No got-um silk-black hat, no stove-pipes hat;
Him got-um plenty-much holes in Washin'ton pants."
Tell-um holes in pants now big, plenty-big—
Bigger dan golden medal on chest!

So much—dat's enough.

How! How!
Kay-gét! Kay-gét!
Ho! Ho! Ho!

Boo-zhóo! Boo-zhóo!
Me, Áh-deek-kóons, I mak'-um big talk.
Me, ol' man; I'm got-um sick on knee
In rainy wedder w'en I'm walk. Ugh!
Me, lak moose w'at's ol',
I'm drop-um plenty toot'!
Yet I am big man! Ho!
An' I am talk-um plenty big! Ho!

Hi-yee! Blow lak moose, ol' man!
Ho! Ho!

Hi-yi! Little-Caribou him talk
Lak Ó-mah-kah-kée, dose Bullfrog:
Big mout', big belly,
No can fight!

Ugh! Close mout', young crazy buck!
You stop-um council-talk,
You go 'way council!
Sit wit' squaw!
You lak little Poh-tóong,
Lak pollywog tad-pole:
No can jump-um
Over little piece mud;
Can only shake-um tail
Lak crazy fool! . . .

Kéetch-ie Ó-gi-má, Big Preshiden',
He got-um plenty t'oughts in head;

Me, Caribou, I'm got-um plenty-good t'oughts,
Got-um plenty-good t'oughts in head.
Yet Eenzhun-Agent all-tam' saying:
"Áh-deek-kóons, he crazy ol' fool!"
Ugh! *He* crazy ol' fool!

Kéetch-ie Ó-gi-má long tam' ago
Was say in Pine Point Treaty:
"All de 'Cheebway should be farmer;
All will get from Washin'ton gov'ment
Good allotment farm land,
One hondred-sixty acre each." Ho!
Ho! Eenzhun scratch-um treaty.
Stick-um t'umb on treaty.

W'at's come treaty? Hah?
Eenzhun got-um hondred-sixty acre,
But got-um too much little pieces—
Pieces scattered over lake
Lak leaves she's blow by wind.
In tam'rack swamp by Moose Tail Bay
He got-um forty acre piece.
Ten mile away, on Lake of Cut-foot Sioux,
In mush-káig an' in swampland,
He got-um forty acre more.
On Bowstring Lake, she's t'orty mile away,
In sand and pickerel weed,
He got-um forty acre more.
Hondred mile away, on Lac La Croix,
W'ere lumberman is mak' big dam
For drive-um log—an' back-um up water

All over Eenzhun allotment land—
He got-um forty acre more—all under lake!
How can Eenzhun be good farmer! Ugh?
He's got-um land all over lake!
He's got-um land all under lake!
For Eenzhun be good farmer
Eenzhun should be good for walking under water!
Should be plow hees land wit' clam-drag!
Should be gadder potato crops wit' fish-net!
For Eenzhun be good farmer
Eenzhun should be fish!
Ugh!

I have said it!

> *Ho! Ho! Ho!*
> *Hi! Hi! Plenty-big talk!*
> *How!*

WEENG

An Indian Slumber-song

Hush! my baby, or soon you will hear
The Sleepy-eye, Wéeng-oosh, hovering near;
Out of the timber he will come,
A little round man as small as your thumb.
Swinging his torch of a red fire-fly,
Out of the shadows old Sleepy-eye,
With the sound of a ghost, on the wind will creep
To see if a little boy lies asleep;
Over your cheeks old Weeng will go,
With feet as soft as the falling snow—
Tip-toe . . . . tip-toe.

Hush! my little one, close your lids tight,
Before old Sleepy-eye comes tonight;
Hi-yáh! if he finds you are still awake,
He draws from his quiver a thistledown stake;
With an acorn for club he pounds on its butt,
Till Sleepy-eye hammers the open eye shut;
Then from his bundle he pulls out another,
Hops over your nose and closes the other;
Up and down with his club he will rap
On the open lid till he closes the gap—
Tap-tap . . . . tap-tap.

If Wéeng-oosh comes at the end of this day,
And finds you asleep he will hurry away . . .

Do you hear him cry on the winds that blow?—
And walk on the earth as soft as a doe?—
To-and-fro . . . . to-and-fro . . .
Hi-yáh! he has crept away from my lap!
For he found my little boy taking a nap.
Oh, weep no more and whisper low,
I hear the feet of Sleepy-eye go—
Tip-toe . . . . tip-toe.

THE BIRTH OF WÁY-NAH-BO-ZHÓO

Long ago, in the hunting-moon
After the muskrat brought between his paws
From the bottom of the sea the piece of mud
That made the beginning of the earth,
There lived a Woman-Who-Was-a-Ghost.
Ho!—she was pretty, as pretty to look at
As a whistling swan, as shy and wild.
She was so beautiful and good
That even the old women of our tribe,
Whose tongues are sharp from too much talking
And clucking between their teeth,
Have nothing to say about her.

All day, all night,
The sun and moon would look at her
And long to put their hands on her;
But their medicine was not strong enough.
Even the big strong gods, the Thunder-bird,
The White Bear, the crafty Coyote,
Hungered for her; and every night
They tried to enter the woman's lodge
And lie down beside her until morning.

> *That is good to think about, my friend—*
> *Ain't?—but for a younger man than I.*

But every night they paced the woods,
Sucked in their breath, and ground their teeth;
For Grandmother Nóh-koh-mís, the Earth,

Circled the wéeg-i-wam all night
And guarded the pretty-one too well,
Like a dog that watches a buffalo-bone;
Grandmother Earth, with the sharp wet nose
And pointed ears of a fox with cubs,
Catching the scent of any sneaking lover,
The crackle of a twig beneath his feet,
Would snarl back her lips upon her teeth,
Shriek to the frightened stars,
And chase him back into the woods
With a big club of iron oak.

When I was a young man, my friend,
I could have given her a good run,
The old hag! No old woman could stop me;
There was no daughter I could not cover,
In the dark of the moon.

Among the lovers were the four windy spirits;
They were too cunning for old lady Nóh-koh-mís.

My son,
Women are women—
Even the best of them.

One night the Spirit-of-the-East-Wind
Crept from the Land-of-the-Morning-Sun;
Softly behind a fog that covered the hills
He stepped, on the still wet feet
Of a quiet little rain;
Softly he crept upon his belly

Into the pretty woman's lodge.
All night he lay beside her
And covered her face with wet kisses.

She did not move a muscle.
The blue sky in her dreams
Did not hold one blur—
Except a little cloud of gray.

> *He was very smart, my friend—ain't?*
> *Rainy weather is always good for stalking.*

Another night the Spirit-of-the-South-Wind,
Floating from the Land-of-Whip-poor-wills,
Came up the valley of the Big-River,
Crawled under the wéeg-i-wam wall
And stretched himself beside her.
With his fingers as soft and warm
As the breeze in the Moon-of-Flowers
He touched her breasts;
With a breath more sweet
Than the air in the Moon-of-Flowers,
When the chokecherry trees are full of blossoms,
He put his mouth to hers.
All night he breathed his sweet warm breath
On the pretty woman while she slept.

She did not move a muscle.
The blue sky in her dreams
Did not hold one blur—
Except a little cloud of yellow-green.

He is always smart with women—ain't?—
This windy-one. When he comes up the valley,
Always in spring, the women
Sing to themselves, sigh every minute,
And go walking all alone in the forest.
When I was a foolish little boy
There was a mystery in this;
But I learned something one day—
From a pair of squirrels;
And after that, when the south wind blew,
I would hide by the forest-trail,
And wait for the girls, and catch them.
They would not struggle much.
I am also smart—ain't?

Another night the Spirit-of-the-West-Wind
Danced on sure feet from the Land-of-Coyotes;
Until the moon swam down the sky
He hid himself among the spruces,
Sighed in the crowns of all the pines,
And made strong songs among the branches.
All evening he blew in the hollow river-reeds
And played upon them as if they were lovers'-flutes;
In the hour before the break of day
He came with dancing feet into the woman's lodge
And pulled her close to him.

She did not move a muscle.
The blue sky of her dreams
Did not hold one blur—
Except a little cloud of vermilion.

She was a heavy sleeper—ain't?—
Like mák-wa, the bear, who holes up
To sleep all winter—Ho!
But that is the way my grandfather told it,
And he knew everything about beginnings—
And his tongue could never talk crooked.

Another night the Spirit-of-the-North-Wind
Came roaring from the Land-of-Big-White-Bears.
Spitting and yelling among the lodge-poles,
With his icy hands he ripped the birch-bark
Flapping on the peak and dropped by the sleeper.
All night he crushed her to his ribs
With his big white twisted arms
And put his hard lips on hers.

She did not move a muscle,
Not even a finger, an eyelid.
The blue sky of her dreams
Did not hold one shadow—
Except a little cloud of white.

That is the way to take a woman—Ho!—
With noise, strong arms, and quick sharp teeth.
But each of the windy-spirits had a way
All his own, and every way was good.

One morning in the Moon-of-the-Suckers
The spirit-woman clapped her hands
Over her mouth; her eyes grew round and white;
For she was heavy with a child to come,

And felt a kicking out of legs.
And Nóh-koh-mís drew back her lips
Over her yellow teeth and smiled;
She knew that only a ghost, a spirit-one,
Could have dodged her eyes and tricked her,
Only a ghost could have been with the lovely-one.

In the Moon-of-Strawberries
The virgin dropped four children on the earth,
Beside a spring, and she was very glad.
One child was like the Spirit-of-the-East;
He had a very solemn face,
Wet eyes that never smiled,
And very quiet hands and feet.
One child was like the Spirit-of-the-South,
Sighing all day and humming softly—
His hands were soft and warm.
One child was like the Spirit-of-the-West,
With quick tough feet,
And a wide big-singing mouth.
One child was like the Spirit-of-the-North—
Bellowing every minute, full of tricks,
And always kicking out with arms and legs.

The four strong windy-ones stretched up
And grew more swiftly than corn-stalks
Fed by much rain and sun;
After forty sleeps they stood
Much taller than their mother—
Ho! bigger than tall smokes.

At sunset, early in the Moon-of-Falling-Leaves,
While their mother was kneeling by a spring,
Filling her birch-bark buckets,
The windy brothers huddled together
In a thicket of bent balsams
And whispered strange things to one another.
Quickly they parted, ran in four directions,
And wheeled to face their kneeling mother.
Together they drew deep breaths,
Puffed out their cheeks together,
And together blew upon the woman—
Big gusts that swirled around her,
That stripped the trees of all their leaves,
And flung a whirling cloud of dust on her.

When the dust and leaves had settled,
And the roaring winds had fallen to a whisper—
Like going thunder after a summer-storm—Ho!—
Nobody, nobody was bending by the spring;
The spirit-woman had vanished from the world,
Like a snow-flake before a sudden sultry wind—
Nobody knows to what strange country
Of spirit-ones she went, nobody can say.

She did not leave one track, one sign,
To show that she had walked this earth—
Except beside the spring a round red spot
Upon the soil where she had given birth
To her four windy children.

On the crimson spot upon the dirt—
As a pine that sends its roots into the soil

From a little seed, and moon by moon,
Stretches itself and reaches to the sky—
So Wáy-nah-bo-zhóo, the mischief-maker,
Fastened himself on earth and grew;
From the crimson spot upon the ground,
Nourished by seven summers of sun and rain
And the milk-dripping breast of Nóh-koh-mís,
Wáy-nah-bo-zhóo drew up his mighty body;
For seven summers more and seven winters
His windy brothers fed him, trained him every day
For jumping, fighting, cunning,
And blessed him with their powers:
Child-of-the-East-Wind built in him
The calmness of rain, still feet for stalking,
And the mystery of quiet-falling rain;
Child-of-the-South-Wind put in him
A warm heart, a tongue for soft sweet talk,
And hands that could be very gentle;
Child-of-the-West-Wind shaped his mouth
For many bright songs, his limber legs
For dancing easily and steadily;
Child-of-the-North-Wind made in him
The strong white bones of winter,
Big shoulders that could crack an oak
As if it were a withered reed,
And put upon his iron lips
The sounding words of blizzards.

What man of blood and bone, my son,
Can wrestle with a child of the four winds?
And of a woman who was a ghost?—

Or talk more big and strong than he?
  Or play more tricks?
  Or be more smart?
  Or more mysterious?
    Nobody . . .
    Nobody . . .

CHANT FOR THE MOON-OF-FLOWERS

On the sacred flame, O Mighty Mystery,
I fling my handful of good red willow bark;
Like willow smoke that floats upon the dusk,
My prayer goes winding up the sky to you:

In the Moon-of-Strawberries-and-Raspberries
Stain the green world, O Maker-of-all-good-things,
With a bursting yield of berries; let them hang
Plenty upon the bush, and heavy with blood.
Let the trout and whitefish walk into my nets
Thick as the stars that swim across the sky;
And may the Big-Knives offer plenty silver
For every catch of fish; ho! let the price
Of fat young pike and trout be seven coppers
No longer—eight is good, and nine is better.
    Not for myself I ask all this,
      But for my little boy, Red-Owl,
        For he is good.

In the Moon-of-Blueberries ask our mother earth
To let the sap go up her stalks of corn
In sparkling currents; make the huckleberries
So plentiful that when we shake the twigs
Above the mó-kuk, the sagging fruit will patter
Down on the birch-bark bucket—round blue rain;
Make the wild hay deep among the meadows,
More soft and thick than winter-fur of beaver,
So thick the north wind cannot part the grasses.

Not for myself I ask these presents,
But for my daughter, Little-Bee,
  For she is good.

In the Moon-of-Changing-Color-of-the-Leaves
Ripen the wild rice growing in the marshes,
Until the yellow grains are full of milk,
Ripe for the world, like heavy-breasted women;
In the wet mush-káigs, make cranberries plentiful,
Thick as the dots that mark the spotted trout;
And may the goose-plums on the tree be many,
So full of clear red honey that they burst
Their skins and spatter sweet upon the earth.
  Not for myself I ask these gifts,
  But for my woman, Yellow-Wing,
    For she is good.

Ho! Mystery, I fling upon the fire
My handful of willow bark to make you glad;
Open your hands and toss me many presents
Showering on the earth like falling leaves.

SPOTTED-FACE, THE TRIBAL FOOL, PRAYS

O Mystery, take my feast of maple-sugar
Set on this medicine-earth for you to eat!—
And let your heart grow good to me with presents.

Give me the legs and sinews of the moose,
For trailing otters steadily from sleep
To sleep; the cunning of the timber-wolf,
That I may kill prime fishers, minks, and martens;
And put upon the pan of my trap the paws
Of silver foxes, and let its ragged teeth
Hold to the bone with the never-ending clutch
Of quicksand—ho! many foxes—eleven, twelve!

All this I ask, that I may pack much fur
To the village—pelts to the muzzle of my gun,
Pelts that will put white eyes in the heads of all
The pretty-colored women, bold round eyes
That burn my spotted face with naked asking.

Put in my hands your devil-magic herbs:
A medicine to kill Blue-Whooping-Crane,
Whose pretty talk, like the tongue of a rattlesnake,
Tickled my woman until she bared her breast
To it and took his poison in her blood;
A medicine to wither and rot the legs
Of Pierre La Plante, who took her to his lodge,
And ran with her to parish Trois Pistoles.

Give me an herb to lock the jaws of women
Tight as a rusty trap, to freeze the lips

Of the dry old women of my tribe who speak
My name with mouths that flow with dirty laughter.

Fix me a woman, a woman who will hold
Herself for me alone, as the trumpeter-swan
That waits through lonely silver nights for wings
That whistle down the wind like an old song.

*Ho! Mighty-Spirit, let your heart grow good
To me with presents; so much I ask—no more.*

THE CONJURER

Come ye, spirits three!
Out of the East, out of the West, out of the North!
Rise ye, má-ni-dó, from your wéeg-i-wams
In the corners of the earth!
Blow, blow, blow thy raging tempests
Through the ranks of whining pine!
Come ye! Come ye to my chée-sah-kán
Riding on thy crazy-running winds.
Hear! Hear my potent chantings!
Bestow me the strength to work my conjurings.
Hi! Take ye my good medicine,
This precious skin of a jumping-rat
Killed in the hour when death,
When clattering death walked into my lodge—
And three moons, three moons dried
On the grave of my youngest son.
Hi! Hear me! Hear me, má-ni-dó!

Come ye, spirits three!
Out of the East, out of the West, out of the North!
Hi! Blow, blow, blow thy whirling winds!
Sway my wéeg-i-wam, sway it
With the breathings of the cyclone!
Hi! Bend its birchen poles
Like the reeds in yonder bay!
Hi! Clutch my wéeg-i-wam, bend it
Till its peak shall scrape the ground!
Hear me! Hear me, má-ni-dó!

How! How!
Behold! my friends, it bends
Like a lily in the storm!

Come ye, spirits three!
Out of the East, out of the West, out of the North!
On the wings of the wind send into my lodge
The lean spirit of a lean coyote—
Of the dying prairie-wolf whose whimperings
We followed many sleeps across the desert.
Make him, má-ni-dó, fling up again
His last long mournful wailings
When thirst and hunger clutched
His withered aching throat—
That the old men of my tribe may hear
Again his ghostly callings as of old.
Hear me! Hear me, má-ni-dó!

How! How!
Ho! There is a power
In my precious ratskin!

Come ye, spirits three!
Out of the East, out of the West, out of the North!
On the wings of the wind send into this lodge
The spirit of Sings-in-the-Hills
Who walked to his death in his birch canoe
Over the falls of the Cut-Foot Waters.
Blow his spirit into my lodge,
That his aged father who sits without
May hear his voice again.

Hear me! Hear me, má-ni-dó!
Make his ghost to talk from my lodge
That the people who watch my juggling
May know his voice again.

How! How!
Hear, my people?
My medicine-skin is strong with power!

Hear ye, spirits three!
Go ye back to thy wéeg-i-wams
In the corners of the earth.
Into the East, into the West, into the North.
Leash again the wolves of the wind. . . .
To thee, O Má-ni-dó of the East,
This handful of burning balsam
Which I fling on the dying wind;
To thee, O Má-ni-dó of the West,
This handful of yellow medicine,
Powder of precious clays;
To thee, O Má-ni-dó of the North,
This red willow twig whereon I have rubbed
My potent medicine ratskin.
Go ye back, ye má-ni-dó,
To the corners of the earth!
Hah-eeee-yóooooooooooo!

How! How!
Enter ye the wéeg-i-wam, my friends!
Unbind ye the basswood cords from my body!
I am done!
How! How!

RAIN SONG

I

God of the Thunders, Thunder-God,
Hear thou our medicine-rattles!
Hear! Hear our sounding drums!
Hi! Our medicine-bag on yonder rock
Has a power, a big-good medicine power—
Three silver scales of the Great Sea Monster—
Ho! Big rain-medicine! Strong rain-medicine! Ho!
Ugh! Behold! On the rock by the stream the Beast
Has placed three scales from his slimy belly—
Ho! Big medicine! Ho! Strong medicine!—
Silver scales of the Big Sea Monster!
Hi! Spirit-of-Thunder, come in thy fury,
Come with thy wet winds, come with thy many waters;
Come in thy wrath against thy foe
That taunts thee there with his filthy poison.
All the children of the earth are good,
Heap-good in the heart to the Thunders;
All the children of the earth are bitter—
Ugh!—bitter to thy foe, the Demon!
We spit!—Behold! we spit on him!
Come with a heart that is good to thy children—
Ho! And big-many waters and heap-much rain!
Come with a heart that is bad to our enemy—
Ho! And big-much lightning, plenty-big storm!
Ho! Silver-wing God, with thy swift wet feet,
Come! Come! Come in thy big black war clouds!
Hurl thy arrows of flashing flame!

Rush at our foe with thy whirlwind waters!
Crush with thy storms the stinking beast
That defies thee here with his slimy poison—
Ho! Big medicine! Ho! Strong medicine!—
Silver scales of the Big Sea Snake!

Ho!

II

Hah-yée! Hah-yó-ho-o-o-o! Hah-yó-ho-o-o-o!
God of the Thunders, Thunder-God,
Hear thou our medicine-rattles!
Hear! Hear our sounding drums!
Two moons the mountain brooks have been dry,
And the panting birds like ghosts in a row,
Perch in the shade and sing no longer.
Our Brother, the Sun, can find his face
No more in the shining-glass of the river;
His eyes see nothing but yellow cracked mud
As wrinkled as the skins of our old women.
Eagerly the sunflower lifts her mouth to the dew,
Yet her lips parch and her head droops,
And her leafy arms grow thin and wither.

Ai-yee! Thunderer, Spirit of the Big Waters,
With burning tongues all the children of the earth—
The flower-people and the hungry grasses,
The sky-flyers and the water-walkers—
All, all are calling, calling, calling to thee.
Hear! Hear our many, many callings!
Hah-yée! Hah-yó-ho-o-o-o! Hah-yó-ho-o-o-o!

138

Thick with hot dust the old men of the forest
Stand with bended heads complaining wearily,
Grumbling ever at the hot winds,
Mumbling ever of the beating sun.
Among the brittle pines the fires run
With many swift feet through the crackling bushes;
And the deer, like whirling leaves in the wind,
Scurry madly before their scorching breath.
The sweet wet grass of our valley-meadows
Is blown by the hot winds into powder;
And our ponies nibble at rustling rushes.
Like the papoose that puts its mouth
To the scrawny breast of an old squaw,
The corn thirstily sucks at the earth—
In the blistered earth there is dust, dust.
And my brothers talk with thick hot tongues,
And my people walk with skinny bellies,
And die like the burning grass of the prairies.

Ai-yee! Thunderer, Spirit of the Big Waters,
With parching mouths all the children of the earth—
The many-foot-walkers and the belly-creepers,
The timber-beasts and the all-over-the-earth-walkers—
All, all are calling, calling, calling to thee.
Hear! Hear their many, many callings!
Hah-yée! Hah-yó-ho-o-o-o! Hah-yó-ho-o-o-o!

III

Háh-yaaaaaaah! Háh-yaaaaaaah!
Háh-yaaaaaaah! Háh-yaaaaaaah!

God of the Thunders, Thunder-God,
Hear thou our medicine-rattles!
Hear! Hear our sounding drums!
Hí-yee! Behind the clouds on the far horizon,
Beat, beat, beat on thy crashing war-drums!
Hí! Hi! Hí! To the war-dance beat,
Shake the earth with thy stamping feet!
Over the fires of the blazing sky
Fling thy blankets of thick wet mist.
Roll from the hills the wet gray fog.
Blow from the hills the cool wet winds.

Hi! Come! Come! Come, thou God of the Thunder!
Come on thy whirling winds from the West!
Come with a rush of thy wings of silver!
Crush our foe with thy tramping feet!
Hí! Hi! Hí! With thy flame-plumed war-club,
Crack the skies in wrath asunder;
And pour from thy hands through thy silver fingers
Cool sweet-waters on the panting earth.
Ho! Wingèd-One of the rumbling rain clouds,
With thy war-drums, sky drums, call thy Water-Spirits.
On thy serpent-foe—we spit on him!—
Let loose thy fire-flashing Thunder.
Ho! Big Tornado! Ho! Thou Cyclone!
Rouse from slumber, dash from the North!
Ho! Big Hand-Walker, who goes head down,
With twirling legs that walk in the sky,
Come over the plains with thy trailing hair
Of tangled winds and twisting rains.

Ho! Thou God of the Thunder-drums,
Pour from thy hands the many-many waters:
Ho! Rains like clouds of silver lances,
Cool long rains that slant from the West;
Rains that walk on gentle little moccasins,
Softly slipping from the fogs in the East;
Cold white rains from the Land-of-Winter,
Dripping in the trees, beating on the birch-bark;
Soft rains, gray rains, rains that are gentle,
Swift rains, big rains, rains that are windy—
Rains, rains, many-many rains.

Hi! Thou God of the Sounding Thunder,
Split the clouds with thy club asunder!
Come! Come! Come with thy stamping feet!
Hí! Hi! Hí! To the war-dance beat!
Bitter in the heart to the Great Sea Monster;
Bitter to our foe; bitter to his poison—
Ho! Big medicine! Ho! Strong medicine!
Silver scales of the Big Sea Snake!

Ho! Ho!

MEDICINE-MAN CONVERSATIONALLY TO THE ASSEMBLED
         TRIBE:

Go to thy wéeg-i-wams, my people.
Already the morning star is high.
Sleep with untroubled hearts.

Come tomorrow to the dancing-ring;
The doctors will then dance the Thanks-Song.
Bring presents—Ho!—and plenty meat!

MEDICINE-MAN BRUSQUELY TO A FELLOW MEDICINE-MAN:

Ugh! Lame-Wolf! . . . Tobacco! . . .
Ugh! . . . I spit on your red willow tobacco!
It has no teeth! It is for squaws!
Give me your white man's tobacco—
The black stick with the stuck-on silver dog! . . .

APPENDIX

THE BOX OF GOD

THE BOX OF GOD

I am moved to speak at some length on "The Box of God," one of the more ambitious pieces in this collection. It would be helpful perhaps to discuss some of the red man's religious beliefs that lie at the foundation of this poem. There is much, no doubt, that could be said, and perhaps should be said, on this narrative, which not only records the conversion of a pagan Indian to Christianity in a mission among the forests north of Lake Superior, but also sets out aspects of the old, old struggle of all the human race, white as well as red, to find the Ultimate, to find God. Such a theme involves so many phases of Indian religion that one could throw light on some of the implications of the poem by discussing the spiritual outlook of the Indian as it is touched upon in this piece. But from another point of view further comment on this poem—beyond the definition of a few strange words—would be futile and inadequate. Some things one cannot say. I shall let the poem itself utter as best it can a portion of what I am moved to express at this moment.

The word "black-robes" for many years was the term used by Indians to indicate a Catholic priest and sometimes a Protestant missionary. The black-robed priests of the Roman Catholic Church were among the first missionaries to carry the gospel to the Indians of America. Undoubtedly they were among the most successful.

145

Contrary to popular belief, among the Indians the common name to designate a white man is not "pale face"—at any rate, not among the tribes I have known. The term used is "Big-Knife." The Chippewa (or Ojibway) Indians use the Chippewa word "Kéetch-ie Móh-ka-món" which means literally "Big Knife." It is obviously a reference to the sabers of the cavalrymen, of the Indian-fighters of the United States Army with whom the Indians of the West and the North came in early contact.

"K'tchée-gah-mee" is the Chippewa word for "Lake Superior." It means literally "Big-Water" or "Big-Lake." It is a corruption of the correct word, "Kéetch-ie Gáh-mee," or "Géetch-ie Gáh-mee" (the consonants "k" and "g"—also "b" and "p" and "d" and "t"—are interchangeable in the Chippewa language—different bands of Ojibways sound them differently). But "K'tchée-gah-mee," the colloquial corruption of the formally correct word, is the word actually used by the red inhabitants of the forests north of Lake Superior.

"Kéetch-ie Má-ni-dó," the central theme of this poem, means "Big Spirit." In the religion of the Chippewa the universe is peopled with many "má-ni-dós," with many spirits or gods. Some of them reside in eagles and bears, others in the four winds, in the sun, in thunder, and there are many other minor spirits. But high above them all, in supreme command, is "Kéetch-ie Má-ni-dó"—the Great Mystery.

The word "Shing-ób" means "spruce." It is the surname of the central character in the narrative—Joe Shing-ób, or Joe Spruce.

"Ah-déek," which means "caribou," is the Indian name given to Joe Spruce's white friend and companion.

"Chée-sah-kée" refers to the "black-medicine-men" who

146

conjure the aid of evil spirits rather than that of good spirits.

The pidgin-English utterances of Joe Spruce in "II: Whistling Wings" are obviously a strange blending of Indian idiom and French-Canadian patois. The origin of this common dialect of the northern Indian may be readily understood when one recalls that the French explorers, fur-traders, and voyageurs long before our nation was established found their way to the wilderness of the Lake Superior region—to what is now Minnesota, Michigan, Wisconsin, and Ontario. Many of the Frenchmen remained among the Chippewas and married into the tribe. As a result, Chippewas have more than a dash of French blood. Many words in the Chippewa language are corruptions of original French words. Consequently, the pidgin-English dialect of the Indian reveals much French influence.

FLYING MOCCASINS

THE SQUAW-DANCE

The songs and dances of the American Indian are almost beyond calculation. Assuredly the complete range and number of them are not known to any white man, or even to any Indian. First, consider the fact that there are many Indian nations and each nation embraces many tribes. These nations and tribes differ somewhat—often much—in their beliefs and practices, in their religion, their music, and their dances. They all have songs and dances peculiarly their own. Furthermore, a single tribe—for example, the Chippewas who dwell chiefly in Minnesota, Wisconsin, Michigan, and Canada—may possess a vast variety of songs and dances: the music and ceremonies of the many medicine-societies; "dream" songs and love songs; "give-away" dances, begging dances, pipe dances, and war-dances; songs for gambling games, for the presentation of gifts, for funerals and mourning; songs for the entertainment of children, for periods of fasting, for curing the sick, for celebrating good harvests, for insuring good crops, good fishing, good hunting—oh, there are many more. But not only every tribe has its vast number of songs and dances but also every individual medicine-man and singer knows and uses songs peculiarly his own. They are his private property, for they came to him in a dream induced by fasting and they involve his private "spirit-helper," the spirit of the particular bear or tree or buffalo who came to him in his dream. No man knows, and no man will ever know, all the songs, dances, and ceremonies of the Indians of America.

In all his music-making the Indian uses only a few instruments: a variety of drums—water-drums, tom-toms, and a huge drum on which several Indians beat simultaneously in the center of the dancing-ring; bells of many kinds, chiefly sleigh-bells, rattles, gourds with pebbles in them or dried substances; and occasionally he uses whistles of hollow bone. In his love songs and serenades the northern woods Indian uses the Bée-bee-gwún, a cedar flute on which he usually plays a simple but wistful tune.

Although there is great variety in the songs and dances of the American Indian, one type of dance is well-nigh universal. It is called the "Squaw-Dance," the "Woman's Dance," or most often perhaps, the "Give-away Dance." Nearly every tribe has preserved some variation of this social dance. But all the variations are basically alike in rhythm, ideas, and spirit. It is a "good-time" dance in which both men and women participate. It is one of the few dances in which women may participate. This is the ceremony upon which the poem "The Squaw-Dance" is built.

"The Woman's Dance" is often held on the Fourth of July, or to celebrate the end of a period of mourning, or for exhibition purposes before white tourists, or at any other time when the band is disposed to have a "good-time dance."

In this performance most of the men and women arrange themselves in a big circle around the group of men beating a big ceremonial drum in the center of the ring. The Indians in the circle shuffle to the left steadily and rhythmically to the beat of the drummers and their lively singing. Within the circle, at the center of the ring, individual men dance robustly. There is occasional laughter, and always there is happiness in this dance. But Indians as a rule tend to be somewhat sober and earnest of countenance when they are enjoying themselves profoundly. As someone has said, they take their fun seriously.

It is customary in this ceremony for some of the Indians dancing in the center of the ring to select a friend in the shuffling circle—or an onlooker—and present a gift to him, a plug of tobacco, a pair of moccasins, a buckskin shirt—I have seen Indians give away their favorite ponies and eagle-bonnets with scores of plumes valued at one dollar a plume. Whereupon the recipient of the gift must dance in the center of the ring with the friend thus complimenting him, and later he must return the honor with a gift of equal value. And thus, with occasional interruptions for the giving away of presents, all day and all night the celebration continues vigorously.

This poem, "The Squaw-Dance," is written from the point of view of an *onlooker*—not of a participant in the dance. I have tried to capture the meaning of the dance, its procedure, and its spirit in order to give the reader a good grasp of what an Indian dance looks like, sounds like, and means. In addition I have preserved accurately the basic rhythm of the "Squaw-Dance" which is characteristic of many other Indian dances. I urge the reader to grasp the rhythm in the poem because it is clearly expressed and easily felt in this piece, and because if he establishes in his ear the rhythm of this poem, he has the key to the basic Indian rhythms in most aboriginal dances.

In reading this dance-poem aloud, the reader should establish and maintain steadily the vigorous beat of an Indian drum which is built into the cadence of the lines. He should depart from this robust drum-rhythm only in the solo-speeches by "Kee-wáy-din-ó-kway" and "Mah-éen-gans" when they bestow their gifts.

THE BLUE DUCK

We said a moment ago that Indian songs and dances are infinite in number—as numerous as grass. Even a single category of Indian music may be beyond classifying. This is especially true of medicine-songs and medicine-dances.

It is difficult to define the word "medicine" as it is used by Indians. It does not necessarily mean ointments and medicines to cure the sick. It is a larger, more inclusive term than this. Some aspects of medicine-making bear upon religion, or mystical supernatural experience. Other aspects involve conjuring, magic, spiritism. And still others involve the use of herbs, objects, and substances which have therapeutic properties in the mind of the Indian. At any rate, the old-time Indian turned to the medicine-man for aid in almost every aspect of life and of living. The medicine-man was at once a priest, a physician, and a conjurer.

The number of medicine-songs and ceremonies is beyond calculation. Every medicine-man possesses not only the common property of songs and rituals given to him as a member of the medicine-society, but he also possesses his own special, potent "medicines," which no other medicine-man may know. As a consequence, there are many kinds of "medicine": medicine to make a good hunting season for the Indian who wishes to trap beavers, minks, martens, fishers;

medicines for curing the lame, the blind, the tuberculous; medicines to bring a curse down on an enemy; medicines to win the love of another; medicines that make for success in war; medicines for mourners and widows; medicines for those who may for any reason wish to commune with the dead; medicines for the period of puberty when boys retire into a remote forest and go into a period of fasting in order to "dream" and in the dream discover their "spirit-helper"; "owl medicine," "rain medicine," and "fire-charm medicine"; and many others, as many as the individual medicine-man in his imagination may create in order to supply the demand of his clients.

"The Blue Duck" is a free interpretation of a hunting medicine-song. It is based on the medicine-making of John Still-Day, at one time the ablest medicine-man on the Red Lake Indian Reservation in Minnesota. Still-Day was regarded as especially effective in making hunting and trapping medicine.

In some medicine rituals it is customary for the medicine-man to carve out of cedar a small image of the person, the animal, or the object which is the central figure in the ceremony or the situation. Thus, for example, in the making of love medicine the conjurer always carves a small image of the person of the opposite sex whom one wishes to captivate, and the image is used in the ritual. In the hunting medicine involved in "The Blue Duck" the medicine-man carves an image of a duck—the central figure in his conjuring; the figure is a symbol about which much of the ritual revolves.

In the medicine-song the medicine-man invokes Kéetch-ie Má-ni-dó, "The Big Spirit," to send down from the North a big flight of ducks for the fall hunt and in general to make a season of good hunting and trapping.

"Kéetch-ie Má-ni-dó," a name which appears frequently in the Indian poems in this book, means literally, "Big Spirit," and, broadly, "The Great Mystery," "God." In the mind of the Chippewa of pagan faith, the world is peopled with many "má-ni-dós," or spirits. These spirits are good and evil. One of the most powerful of them lives in the bear— the Mák-wa Má-ni-dó. A very good spirit lives in the green frog. An old pagan Indian will never hurt a green frog; he will look at you aghast if you fasten one on a barbed hook as bait for a bass. One of the most evil má-ni-dós lives in the little red frog who makes his home in the rotten stumps of trees. Another evil spirit is "Mú-chie Má-ni-dó"; he resembles somewhat the white man's devil. There are five spirits stronger than these, however; four of them are the spirits who live in the points of the compass and in the four winds, North, East, South, and West; the fifth is the god called "Thunderbird." These five great spirits, however, are merely lieutenants of "The Big Spirit." Above all these minor deities rules "Kéetch-ie Má-ni-dó."

In the oral rendition of "The Blue Duck," the reader should establish a robust up-and-down drum-beat rhythm in the first few lines and adhere to it steadily, except when the poem rises to the level of a chant, or a wail, or a prayer.

THUNDERDRUMS

This poem is a free interpretation of a war-medicine ceremony performed often in the old days of the Chippewas as a part of their preparations for war with the Sioux, their bitter enemies. The ancient war-dance has been preserved by some of the tribes and is performed occasionally by the Red Lake Chippewas.

A brief description of a war-dance and a study of the poem, "Thunderdrums," will reveal the futility of translation as a method of capturing the ideas and the spirit of Indian songs and dances.

In the war-dance while the chiefs and the braves danced in the ring for long periods and worked themselves into a high emotional pitch in preparation for a battle, the medicine-men made war-medicine. By means of their chants and their "good medicines" they would render the warriors immune from injury and death; they would invoke the aid of the powerful spirits, especially the spirit of the Thunderbird. They would endow the tribal warriors with uncommon powers, and thus strengthen the fighting hearts of the braves. The ceremony might continue for hours, yet in the entire period few specific words would be uttered, beyond an exultant *"Ah-hah-háy!"* or *"Háh-yah-ah-háy!"* or a defiant war-whoop, or a blood-curdling shout. Yet consider all that occurred: long periods of dancing, of dramatic posturing, and pantomime, of singing and drumming which varied from time to time in idea and spirit; periods of meaningful medicine-making and invocations. A literal translation of the few words uttered in this dance would reveal little.

But this is not all. In the course of the dance individual braves would perform solo dances. By means of gesture, posture, and pantomime one Indian would enact a dramatic scene; he would tell the story of a former battle in which he had killed an enemy in a hand-to-hand struggle. Another

Indian would portray in his dance-pantomime how he planned to trail, attack, and destroy his foes. A third might impersonate animals or men and horses wounded in battle, or he might enact a score of dramatic incidents relevant to the war-medicine dance. In "Thunderdrums," Sections II-V, "Double-Bear Dances," "Big-Sky Dances," "Ghost-Wolf Dances," and "Iron-Wind Dances," I have sought to capture the spirit of four solo dances or pantomimes typical of many others in the old war-medicine ceremonies.

The dance-pantomime is the root of Indian drama. It is the only form of drama known to the early American Indians, with the exception of certain seasonal dances and ambitious religious ceremonies—and most of these ceremonies are simply elaborations of the more common dance-pantomimes.

The Thunderbird, mentioned often in this poem, is easily one of the most powerful of all the spirits in the supernatural world of the red man. He plays an important role in the conjuring of medicine-men. The Thunderbird comes to the world in electric storms; he manifests himself when the black clouds gather on the horizon, when the sky rumbles with thunder, and the flaming bolts and jagged lightnings flash overhead.

The word "Cut-throat" is the term used by Chippewas occasionally to characterize the Sioux Indian. The word "Pucker-skin" is sometimes used by the Sioux to describe the Chippewa. Chippewa moccasins were fashioned out of buckskin with seams that puckered peculiarly. Hence the name.

The expressions *Ho! Hó!*, *Ah-hah-háy!*, *Háh-yah-ah-háy!*, and *Wuh!* are typical Chippewa explosives and ejaculations of approval and enthusiasm by the audience. The war-medicine dance is peppered with them from the first beat of the drum to the last. Since they represent high peaks of emotion, moments when one cannot find words to express one's feelings, these grunts and shouts are usually blood-stirring in a real war-dance.

The rhythm of the poem is peculiarly Indian; it is the drum-beat rhythm most basic and common among the Chippewa Indians. In the oral rendition of the poem it is imperative that the reader establish at once this vigorous up-and-down drum-beat rhythm and maintain it steadily and robustly throughout the piece. If the reader grasps and renders the vigorous and persistent drum-beat cadence of this poem, he will have the rhythmic key to most of the Indian dance-poems in this book.

INDIAN LOVE SONG

The love songs of the Indian and the love serenades played on the cedar flute are as a rule plaintive in spirit. "Indian Love Song" is typical of the spirit of most Indian love songs and it suggests their characteristic ideas.

INDIAN SLEEP SONG

In the lodges of the more remote Indians one may still see Indian cradle-boards and hear old Indian lullabies. The "tík-in-áh-gun," or cradle-board, is made of basswood on which the Indian baby is bound with beaded cloth and buckskin. This board serves as a cradle and a carrying-board. When a mother wishes her baby to fall asleep, she improvises a hammock from blankets swung between two lodge-poles, places in it the cradle-board to which the baby is lashed, and she sings while she swings the hammock to and fro.

The lullabies of the Indian mother are in spirit much like those of the white mother, except that perhaps they are more plaintive and they usually contain few words—other than the syllables "Wáy-way-wáy" or "Wé-we-wé" or some variation of these. In "Indian Sleep Song" I have endeavored to capture the spirit of a typical Indian lullaby, and the rhythm of a swinging cradle-board.

CRAZY-MEDICINE

One of the medicines in demand among Indians, even today, is "revenge medicine." If an Indian seeks revenge against an enemy or a hated rival, he will probably go to a medicine-man who may select an incantation known as "crazy-medicine." In making "crazy-medicine," the conjurer carves a small cedar image of the foe of his client as large as a man's finger, and on a string he suspends it from an arched willow switch, so that the image may toss and spin freely in the wind. Touching its head with vermilion medicine-paint, he addresses the image as if it were his client's enemy in the flesh. The poem, "Crazy-Medicine," expresses the ideas behind the symbol, behind the conjuring, and in the mind of the medicine-man.

Most Indian love songs express the spirit of loneliness, wistfulness, and melancholy. Sometimes they are somewhat romantic and idealistic in their form of utterance. The circumstances which usually attend the singing of love songs and the playing of serenades on the Bée-bee-gwun make for a romantic setting; the young buck often slides out into the lake in a birch-bark canoe at dusk, or on a moonlight night, and he plays his cedar flute for some young woman back in the village. The picture is pretty. But behind the idealized picture the spirit of love in the heart of the young man is very old, very real, and somewhat elemental.

The poem, "Beat Against Me No Longer," does not reflect the most common type of idealized Indian love song, or the spirit of the melancholy romanticized cedar flute theme, or the ideas most typical of love songs—"I am lonely—thinking about you—weeping for you"; but it does capture the love song in the heart of the Indian, the more realistic spirit that governs the hearts of most Indians in their love making.

The lines beginning, "Be not as the flat-breasted squaw-sich . . . who hides three sleeps in the forest," refers to an Indian custom that requires a girl approaching adolescence, manifesting the first signs of coming womanhood, to leave the village and live alone in a wigwam in the woods for a period.

COUNCIL-FIRES

THE WINDS OF FIFTY WINTERS

The council-oratory of the Indian is interesting in its range and variety. Naturally the beauty and power of any council-talk depends largely on the character of the speaker, on his imagination, on his intelligence, and on other personal traits. Some Indian orators are most effective; others are dull—they drool and drawl in their speaking, exactly as some white speakers do. But on the whole Indian council-speaking offers a fascinating study. Those things peculiarly Indian in the red man shine out most clearly in his council-speaking: his simplicity; his talent for irony; his vivid imagery; his basic dignity; his earthiness; and his genuine power.

In order to provide a scenic background for this group of council-talks, I wish to describe a typical council. A council is a more or less official gathering of Indians for the purpose of determining matters of tribal concern and of formulating tribal policies. It is a place for debating and discussing tribal legislation. It is a thoroughly democratic institution—except that it is usually dominated by the chiefs and the old men whose wisdom and mandates are invariably respected by the tribe. In the old days councils were called often between different tribes in order to settle their differences or for friendly visitations. Sometimes they were held between Indians and white men—usually officers in the United States Army—in order to make treaties.

In recent years, however, the most important councils are

called to iron out tribal difficulties with our government. Al-though the Indians of today are citizens of the United States, most of them are wards of our federal government. Their affairs are supervised and administered in part by the United States Department of the Interior through the Office of Indian Affairs. Whenever this agency of the government wishes to investigate tribal conditions, complaints, or problems or to confer with Indians on the formulation of new tribal policies, a council is called. The Indians in attendance may number a few dozen or several hundred. At this meeting spokesmen for the Indians—usually chiefs and headmen —state their cases through official interpreters to the representative of the Department of the Interior. A court reporter records the speeches as they are interpreted and later they are filed in Washington.

The councils are usually marked by dignity, orderliness, and seriousness. The audience is usually attentive and respectful. It is on the whole undemonstrative except for an occasional expression of approval. In most of the council-poems I have indicated the typical Chippewa exclamations of approval and linguistic applause by inserting them in the poems.

"The Winds of Fifty Winters" is a poetic version of a famous Chippewa council-talk which is spoken of as a classic among old Chippewa Indians. It is recalled always with a chuckle.

MEDALS AND HOLES

For many reasons this poem and most of the other council-talks were written in the broken pidgin-English which a not too civilized and pretentious mixed-blood interpreter at a council would use, rather than in the linguistically elegant language of the white man's formal oratory. Too often official interpreters who have translated addresses made in government councils, historians who have recorded famous Indian orations, and novelists and playwrights who have sought to capture Indian speech, have lost much of the flavor of genuine Indian oratory. In their desire to intensify the romantic element or to make the speech of the Indian more easily comprehended by the white man often they have fallen back on the formal rhetoric of the white man. As a result, our recorded Indian speeches are sometimes too formal, too studied, too elegant and heroic. The few examples of Indian oratory available in the English language are sometimes more white man than Indian in spirit. The genuine beauty of his speech, its simplicity and naïveté, its broad and subtle humor, its moments of grandeur, its earthiness and brute power— these have been too often smothered and lost in rhetorical elegance and ornamentation.

Moved, therefore, by a desire to preserve the less romantic but perhaps more vital aspects of his speech, I offer this council-talk and most of the other council-talks with the hope that their loss in fluency and polish which results from the broken dialect in which they are written may be offset by their gain in spontaneity and naturalness, in ruggedness and sense of reality, and in the beauty of stark truth.

The frequent references to "the golden medal" go back to the days when the Kéetch-ie Ó-gi-má, the "Big Chief" of the white man, the President of the United States, seeking to win the friendship and the support of influential chiefs, often awarded them big medals. Indians are usually naive in their love of honors and ornaments. Therefore they prized the medals presented them by the government; the medals were big, gleaming, impressive.

LITTLE-CARIBOU "MAKES BIG TALK"

This poem is based on a council-talk I heard about 1910 at Cass Lake, Minnesota, given by a weazened old man. His speech was typically Indian in its humor, in its wryness, and in its spirit in general.

Many white folk believe that the Indian lacks a sense of humor; that he never laughs or jokes; that he is always the taciturn and sullen red man of the theatre, the circus, the cinema. Many believe, too, that all the ideas he possesses and all the emotions he experiences may be expressed in one word: "Ugh"! How amusing!—and false! True, in formal meetings and in his dealings with the white man the Indian is usually solemn and reserved. But among his own people and in the circle of his family he laughs often and much. Moreover, the women and children seem to be forever laughing, joking, and giggling over nothing. Among the older folk in every Indian tribe are many droll characters, men who possess at once Indian dignity and reserve and a rare sense of humor. The poem, "Little-Caribou 'Makes Big Talk' " deals with this little known side of the Indian.

In council-meetings and elsewhere as a rule the red man is deferential and courteous to elderly people. In this poem, therefore, the jibes and interruptions by the young Indians and the "asides" and the colloquy between Little-Caribou and his young hecklers (represented by the indented stanzas in italics) are unusual.

RED GODS

WEENG

Like white folk, Indians have trouble persuading their children to go to sleep at night. But the Chippewa Indian has an advantage over the white man; he has the assistance of a god who has charge of children and of sleep. His name is "Wéeng-oosh" or "Weeng." He is a spirit no larger than one's thumb. Even in this modern day, in many Indian homes in the north woods at night one may see an old grandmother take over a child who is fighting slumber and put him to sleep with a story or a song about "Wéeng-oosh." The poem "Weeng" is a slumber-song based upon the legend of old "Sleepy-eye," "Wéeng-oosh."

In the oral rendition of this poem the reader should chant the lines quietly and monotonously with the slow sing-song rhythm that marks most of the lullabies of the white man and of the Indian.

THE BIRTH OF WÁY-NAH-BO-ZHÓO

Wáy-nah-bo-zhóo is an important legendary character among the Chippewa Indians. The prowess of this strange, inconsistent hero is set out in scores of folk-tales. He emerges from these many myths a self-contradictory, unbelievable half-god: he is at once angelically good and devilishly bad; he is gentle and he is cruel; he is guileless and he is cunning.

163

An explanation for his caprices and his inconsistencies may be found in this broad interpretation of the legend of the birth of Wáy-nah-bo-zhóo.

The short, indented stanzas which record the "asides" of the narrator of the legend suggest an interesting aspect of some Indians: the sharp contrast between the beauty and power of the Indian in his official character as a medicine-man, an orator, or a teller of folk-tales and the earthy reality of the Indian as a simple human being. In the latter character the red man often has a salty savor and a pungence, like broiled venison.

CHANT FOR THE MOON-OF-FLOWERS

Many prayers, chants, and songs of the woods Indians involve as part of their ritual tossing on the fire a bit of kinnikinic, an Indian tobacco made of red willow bark. The ascending smoke goes up to the Big Spirit and carries the prayer of the Indian. This common ritual lies at the base of this chant for good crops.

SPOTTED-FACE, THE TRIBAL FOOL, PRAYS

Often Indian chants, ceremonies, and council-talks contain a strange blending of the idealistic and the realistic, of the sublime and the crass. This chant illustrates the fairly common practice of combining these incongruous elements.

The word "medicine" is a broad, ambiguous word in the Indian language. It may mean anything from "herbs" to "conjuring," from "magic," to "religion." There are many kinds of medicine and several types of medicine-man. One type which is rapidly disappearing is the "chée-sah-kée," the conjurer, the medicine-man who is in league with bad spirits rather than with good spirit-helpers. He is in a sense a conjurer and a spiritualist. He performs several remarkable feats of magic.

His chief performance, however, is that of conjuring the spirits of the dead into his wéeg-i-wam, or "chée-sah-kán." Several Indians with personal problems that require the help of "the spirits," or who for any of a dozen reasons wish to speak with the dead, may ask the "chée-sah-kée" to "make medicine" for them.

At a designated time the Indians go to the woods with the "chée-sah-kée," and he builds a wéeg-i-wam of birch-bark and stout lodge-poles which are planted so firmly in the earth that they cannot be moved easily by a human being. The "chée-sah-kée" builds a fire before the lodge, squats before the flame, beats his drum and begins to chant. Soon or late the lodge begins to sway gently from right to left. It increases steadily in the vigor of its movements until bells tied to the peak of the lodge-poles begin to jingle. These signs indicate that "the spirits" are within the chée-sah-kán, or lodge, and are ready to communicate with anybody in the circle of Indians who may pose problems and ask questions. The onlookers who had asked the medicine-man to "make chée-sah-kán" and to produce the spirits talk one by one with their favorite spirits—the spirit of a dead relative, or of an animal "má-ni-dó."

If a conjurer ever fails to set the lodge to dancing and to fill the lodge with spirits ready to talk, it is not the fault of his religion or medicine; it means simply that a rival of his is defeating him or some jealous spirit is working against him.

My old Indian friend, Áh-zhay-waince, "Other-Side," a medicine-man of the Pigeon River Reservation, used to per-form this feat. I saw him cause his lodge to rock violently with spirits one night in the deep woods of the Canadian border north of Lake Superior, and I heard the voices of the spirits of dead Indians, of an otter, a beaver and a bear speak from within the lodge. They all spoke the Chippewa lan-guage. The many voices were marked by the same vocal timbre. All the speakers had the same dialectic eccentricities and inflections. Obviously the performance was a clever piece of conjuring, a baffling trick that involved an accomplice. But to most old-time Indians it is no trick; it is "good medi-cine."

"The Conjurer" is a free interpretation of the chant of the Chée-sah-kée and of the performance. The short, indented lines and stanzas in the poem are the conjurer's "asides" to his Indian audience.

RAIN SONG

This interpretation of a medicine-song for making rain is based on an old Indian superstition. During the medicine ritual a buckskin sack containing small mica-like scales is placed on a boulder by a stream near the scene of the ceremony. These bits of mica—"rain medicine"—are believed to be scales from the body of the legendary Great Horned Sea Monster. It is believed that if these scales are exposed during the ritual, the Thunderer and his allies the Thunder-Spirits and the Rain-Spirits, who loathe the Sea Monster, will come with the fury of their storms and clouds and rains to attack their traditional enemy who dares to lift his head out of the stream and to expose a part of his body to the gaze of the Thunder-Beings.

INDEX

INDEX OF FIRST LINES

172

INDEX OF TITLES

DUE TO BE
RETURNED

on last date below. RENEWAL
granted only when transaction
No. and date due given.

Transaction No.	Date Due
2 Jan'	

DATE DUE

12/7/99			

#47-0108 Peel Off Pressure Sensitive